Club Medusa

Club Medusa, Volume 1

Martin White

Published by Martin White, 2020.

CLUB MEDUSA

First edition. May 28, 2020.

Copyright © 2020 Martin White.

ISBN: 979-8223145141

Written by Martin White.

Table of Contents

For my fellow author, musician, ghost hunter and brother,
Steven James White

1968 – 2020

ACKNOWLEDGMENTS

Special thanks to the following fantastic and talented people for helping me get this story out into the world: Kirsty White, Colin Brown, Matthias Bodner, James Ingham and Steven Hassan for eagle eyed editing, Amanda Nicoler and Swords and Scythes for top beta reading, Nik from Bookbeaver for the stunning cover, also to my friends Andy McCaw and Deborah Chalmers for the lowdown on those two vital components for any good night out, alcohol and anaesthetics. Heartfelt thanks also to my amazing family, Kirsty, Logan, Lyra and Zander.

1. Prologue

What do you really matter? Think about that.

There are almost eight billion people alive right now; how many of them do you really care about? How much do you think the rest of them care about you? Be honest.

The fact is, most of us come and go from this life unknown. We live in clusters and layers dictated by chance, luck and money—and none of those layers matter to anyone looking down from the top. Even if you put yourself in harm's way to protect others, making that world safer for them, you're still nothing more than fodder—expendable and consumable.

You can throw around all the first world, social media-friendly slogans you like, but nothing will change the fact that we're all on our own here, and the only things that might save you becoming part of the food chain are birthright and whatever club you might happen to belong to.

Sorry, does all this sound harsh? Nihilistic? Maybe it is, but I promise you it's true.

You probably think you're safe right now but trust me, you're never safe. What about all those people you just admitted you don't care about, the ones skirting around your life, looking at your money, watching everything you do online, listening to you through devices in your home, logging everything you buy at the supermarket? What about the ones walking or driving past you on the street, drinking next to you in the bar, standing around the edge of the dance floor in the club? You don't know them. Believe me, you have no idea what 'other people' are really capable of.

And if none of us really matter, that makes our world a very dangerous place...

2. Plan

I used to believe blame was just a waste of time. Everybody knows bad things happen to good people every day–nothing will change that. But if we *learn* from all these bad things then we can move on, right? All very grown up. I don't think like that anymore, the blame for *this* bad thing belongs to Gerry.

As plans go, his proposition seemed simple and harmless enough. I would take the bus into central Edinburgh and meet him in London Road. We would both then walk into the Old Town via Greenside, visit a couple of old haunts, drink beer and reminisce about the old days. We would be careful not to mention the war (or wars or any past military experiences) throughout, and then we would go home. In that order. It would have been just like any one of countless other plans that night drawn up by friends who wanted to catch up over a beer. Although maybe with the exception of the 'war' clause.

Gerry and I had known each other since way back, we were like two kids that life always just seemed to throw together. We lived near each other when we were kids, went to both the same schools, took a lot of the same knocks as teenagers, ended up joining the military together and eventually ended up serving in the same unit abroad. It genuinely seemed as if we couldn't get rid of each other.

In short, we had travelled through life by way of a lot of the same rough roads, but somehow managed to stay mates through both good and bad. Especially the bad.

Of the bad, our army days were probably the worst. But, had you asked me when I was sitting on the bus on my way into town that night, I probably would have told you the worst of those days were now safely behind us, the army having honourably discharged us both a couple of years earlier. It hadn't been part of any long-term plan, it was more thanks to an operation in Afghanistan which went tits up and turned the pair of us into shrapnel magnets. But that's a story for later.

By the time I was on that bus, we were both mostly used to the civilian life. We were older, arguably more sensible and pretty much getting the hang of what people did in the real world. We knew we had to be grownups, but with that came grownup problems. For example, the catalyst for our catch up that night was because Gerry wanted to offload about a relationship breakup. He had just been dumped by Melanie, the latest in a long line of girls who had probably seen his potential, but couldn't quite manage to get him over himself or his past. Not that I'm judging, it hadn't been so long since I had found a relationship of my own where daily life seemed to work, despite my own past ghosts.

Basically, because we had been out of the loop for so many years playing at soldiers, we both felt as if we were playing catch-up with the world to a certain extent. We both knew if we ever wanted to have 'normal' lives we should be getting a move on as we were already in that 'late thirtysomething' zone and well past our crazy primes, regardless of whatever shit we might shoot over a few beers.

Even in those last two years or so of civilian life, our social trajectories were already showing signs of slowing; our tally of check ins and catch-ups had already dwindled. Maybe one of the reasons was me; I finally seemed to be getting to that place I thought I wanted to be in life. There were even occasions in my own newfound stability where I found I had to check myself for getting all judgmental, usually as I was left holding Gerry's jacket while he flounced off towards the ladies trying to cultivate some fantasy shagfest for himself. Something I would have to say, he rarely succeeded in.

I had never been that way inclined, and thankfully Nik understood that. Nevertheless, even through that understanding, I began to sense her own mounting level of disapproval about alcohol fuelled late nights out in town.

So yes, maybe I did exaggerate the importance of giving my mate a sympathetic shoulder to pretend to cry on that night. Maybe that does mean some of the blame belongs to me. But not much.

*

It was a Friday in late October and the rain had been threatening all day. Even in the streetlit late evening there was still a sense that rainclouds were lurking ominously, just waiting to drop their lot. Gerry had already finished his shift at the hospital earlier that evening where his job as a porter served almost exclusively to pay the silly money gym fees he needed to keep himself muscle-laden and perma-tanned. I met him as planned outside his gym club on London Road. I hadn't seen him in a while and he looked well. He was standing right outside the front door and clearly saw me on the approach.

"Hey mate, how are you? Still on the sex offenders register then?" he asked loudly, which did the opposite of impressing two young girls walking into the club. I shrugged and looked resigned while he suddenly lunged forward and bear hugged me. All very manly.

"You're still an arse then?" I said.

"And yet, a finely taut and attractive one," he replied smugly. I gave in and laughed.

We did the whole insulting banter thing for a bit and then ran through the plan for the evening, even though it was basic. Old habits die hard.

"All fine by me," I said. "And you've been launched by yet another fine woman too? How the hell did you manage that?"

He looked as if he was about to tell me before I cut him off, "No—no—don't tell me yet, we'll get a couple of beers in first, eh?"

He shrugged and smiled, we probably both knew what had happened there anyway. There was also something else I had to ask him, formal housekeeping, "Okay, let's get this over with early doors—how are you coping with, you know—the old stuff?" He knew what I meant, suddenly looking more focused.

"Yeah. Not bad. I'm okay. Still have my moments but—you know, I'm on a level. Sleeping most nights, off most of the meds now. Way better than I was. Yourself?"

"Yeah, I'm good. I know it's all there but I don't get much grief from any of it these days. It all takes time, you'll get there."

We gave each other that look. Like most ex-forces guys, we had left our previous lives with a certain amount of baggage that couldn't just be dropped as easily as we (and everyone else in our lives) would like. Gerry had been through a really bad time with it, although I had stuck around and helped him through the worst—as you do with your mates.

"You remember the drill with the old stuff though?" I said.

"Please don't tell me you're going to make me say it out loud?' said Gerry.

"You know the rules—we don't speak about that stuff in public. We can't, even if it's hurting. Too much drink, loud places, flapping ears, gung-ho idiots and the way the world is right now, okay?"

"Okay, I know. The Code," he sighed.

I nodded, "The Basil principle, don't mention the war."

He shook his head as if I was patronising him.

"Any war," I added.

He shrugged non-committedly; I needed more than that.

"I'm serious, if you want to talk about that stuff, you know I'm here, and I'm all ears—but there's a time and a place for that kind of talk, and it's not out there amongst the drunken civvies. Are we good with that?"

"Uh, yes sir. Okay sir, you overdecorated cock." He paused, glared at me, and then broke into a stupid grin.

"Screw you. We've both got all the same gongs anyway," I said, "and don't diss all the nice colours, they're pretty."

He laughed, we were good, and the message had been received painlessly. We shrugged the serious interlude off, as guys tend to do.

There was one more thing, "Oh, have you got your mobile phone by the way?"

He looked at me as if I was sectionable.

"Are you serious?" he said, 'Why would I have one of those things on me?"

"Good man," I said. It might have been a paranoid hangover from our past, but being visible from space to anyone who wanted to know where you were and what you were doing wasn't my idea of being off the grid for the night. Plus, they were annoying.

We quickly covered the short walk through the late evening pubbers in Greenside Place, up towards Princes Street and then across the North Bridge. Before long we found ourselves at the junction with the High Street, or, the 'Royal Mile', outside our first nostalgia stop, the Bank Bar. Standing opposite the shell of the high steepled Tron Church, the Bank had an impressive sandstone façade and looked as if it may well have been a proper bank at some time. But to us it had always been a starting point, a place for the first and most sober talk of the evening. Also, it had the strategic advantage of being central, so whatever we decided, we could move off into any part of the city centre without too much of a hike.

It was busy when we walked in, suits and smart casual all around, hints of after work and football chat in the air. No one gave us a second glance as we ordered a couple of beers and sat ourselves down at an empty table. We didn't exist to them, which might have seemed unfriendly—but it was fine by me.

And so, on to the formal declared business of the night. I listened dutifully over that first beer as Gerry gave me the story; a tragic, one-sided tale of how his latest relationship's last straw had come about. I made all the right noises as he described the melodrama step by step. As I remember, the script was similar to previous episodes where it had all been great at first but then the poor girl moved in with him and then Gerry's priority to look after himself first became contentious.

There were some faux comedy moments along the way where Melanie decided to restock his wardrobe with more 'age appropriate' clothing when he was at work, and an incident where she'd given all his old vinyl away to a charity shop as it was 'getting dusty'—but overall, it didn't sound as if the girl stood a chance. A dual ultimatum had been given where Gerry insisted she should stop trying to change him or she would have to leave—and she countered this by insisting he should 'grow up' or else she would have to leave. Or whatever.

Either way, the common factor seemed to be Melanie leaving, and leave she did. And also, as I'd suspected, Gerry didn't really appear to be overly upset by it all. I was glad, I had to watch for that. In fact, life changing though this apparently may have been for him during the conversation, I'm guessing he spent all of about fifteen minutes on the subject of the break-up, probably the entirety of his first pint.

Was he putting a brave face on it? Of all the people, I knew how to read him and I could tell he was probably more hurt than he would admit. There were occasional pauses of uncertainty and sometimes he would let the words 'I suppose...' hang off the ends of his sentences—but he didn't seem like a man on the edge. Or anywhere near one for my money. We both knew he just wasn't in a place yet where he could face the attachment and commitment, it was as simple as that. So ultimately, he got what he wanted—his freedom, but probably at the price of moving forward in life. At least, that was the way I saw it.

So, there was no need to worry—he was stable. He was disappointed yes, but not a man in emotional freefall. In fact, as the time passed and the beers progressed, he made his thoughts pretty obvious that we should be finishing our evening off with post-midnight beer in a place where he might find some young, impressionable female company.

And that's where I came in. As I said, if there's any blame for the way that night turned out, it belongs to Gerry. I might have been complicit in going out for those few drinks, but Nik, my own partner, was already less than impressed with being neglected in favour of one of my manfriends on a Friday night, regardless of the drama. Plus, I had to get in to work the next morning...

"Oh, come o*nnnnn*," Gerry drawled over the muted conversation and the music, "This place is full of married women—of both sexes—and it's way too bloody pretentious. Look at them. They're even dressed the same, all that beach rustic pastel with their bloomin' craft beer and cocktails, sitting in their cliques swipin' at their phones. And that fucking jazz drone in the background is doing my nut in."

I couldn't disagree. We may have been sitting quietly at our table, but as the place had become busier, to the rest of the clientele we must have looked as if we were from a different planet. Our leather jackets, jeans and Gerry's worn combats probably ensured that if we were even noticed at all, it would be because we were suspected carriers of the ned-plague by the lot who seemed to have moved in and made this place their own. I made hesitant noises but Gerry was relentless.

"The nightclubs, that's where it's all at now," he said. "'Juice' is on down in the Cowgate, 'Inferno' in Moray House, you know, even The Kitchen or The Attic down the road? Look Paul, you boring old bastard, I just want to get a bit of dancing in, you know? Find a bit of a distraction for the night? Hey, look at me, I'm upset..."

He was a zoomer more like. That had not been part of the plan. I couldn't help but see the consequences if we went there; me falling home drunk and penniless at 4 a.m., a dehydration headache and argument before leaving for work, and then feeling and smelling like shit for the rest of the day. No thank you.

"Oh come o*nnnn*, I just want to celebrate being a free man again. You don't even have to get involved, I can do the thing where I talk you up as my straight acting gay cousin so you don't lose any cred? Just tag along till we find some girls to talk to, then I'll take over and you can leave, honest!"

There was now a whine of desperation in his voice, and I knew from experience that Gerry was notoriously stubborn with a few drinks inside him. It was beginning to look as if there would be no easy way out. But who knows, maybe there was a part of me that still wanted to be able to play like that too?

"Not part of what I signed up for, mate," I said, realising my heart probably wasn't in the argument.

"Come on ya pussy, what's the worst thing that could happen?"

At that time, we had no idea.

Stupidly, I relented. I deviated from the agreed plan, thinking I could improvise later.

"Well, okay. But this is for your benefit, understand? I'll be in a world of shit for being out after twelve and believe me I *will* be going home early enough to get a decent sleep before work."

Gerry beamed triumphantly; he didn't give a shit.

"Ha—good man!" he said, giving me way too heavy a slap on the shoulder which sent me lurching forward in my seat, "You won't regret it. I'm telling you mate, we're both still too young to get written off yet!"

We finished our drinks and left the table. Our places were quickly snapped up by two late twenty-something well-dressed couples who had been hovering nearby. I was aware they were watching us, they had been on my radar since I noticed the odd indignant glare from them, presumably for taking up a table for four when there were only two of us.

As we stood up I smiled at them politely by way of acknowledgement, but was given a look of bitter distaste in return, as they skirted around, urgently filling our seats.

"About time too," I heard one of the girls mutter under their breath. Yeah, you're welcome. Even back then I was pretty intuitive and there was definitely a hostile vibe from this lot, aimed solely at us. I couldn't help glancing back at them again once or twice as we headed for the exit. For some reason both the guys were holding my gaze as we walked away, as if to say, 'Yeah, this stink eye is for you'. Probably just showing off for the ladies, but still, I couldn't be doing with attitude like that. I'm not one for feeling entitled but they clearly had no idea what Gerry and I had willingly put ourselves through just so their arses could safely sit on those seats and their lives could just keep on ticking over peacefully.

I shook my head, broke off eye contact and trailed off behind Gerry towards the door. As we reached the exit, Gerry turned, also looking back to our table; I guessed he had also caught the exchange.

"Aww look, that's so considerate, they're letting GCHQ know where they are."

I glanced back and saw all four were now settled in, each one engrossed in looking at their phones.

"I think we've definitely lost something as a species," he said.

When we stepped outside I felt the humidity had risen, the rain was still on its way. Gerry took a breath and looked thoughtful; I could tell I was going to regret agreeing to his nightclub idea. We stood on the street corner in the moment, looking up at the lit façade of the building we had just left.

"So, is it just me," I asked, "or have people in general just changed for the worse since we first started doing this?"

"Uh? How d'you mean?" Gerry replied, his focus now clearly beginning to shift.

"Well, it's not the same is it? I mean, did you see that lot on their phones? I see it every time I'm out in town. It's as if speech has totally gone out of fashion now that people can just message each other—nightlife just has a very different feel to it now. I mean, please stop me if I sound like an old fart, but when we were the young guys doing the rounds, there weren't many places that would make you feel a total outsider like that, especially in the city centre. Even if you weren't known, there was usually a bit of banter to be had, a bit of a way in."

"Please stop Paul, you sound like an old fart," said Gerry, "Besides, they're all on facey-gram and twatter or whatever. These days it's easy, knobs can find other knobs to hang with without even having to speak to each other."

He turned away; I could tell he was now preoccupied assessing our next move. That passive aggressive displacement had riled me more than it should, but I could see Gerry was well past it; his mind had moved on. It was already dancing under the strobe lights somewhere with some lithe, young brunette.

As we stood on the street corner, Gerry made a show of looking up at the steeple clock of the Tron Church and then at his watch.

"Okay, it's five past one now," he said, "The licencing curfew starts at half past, so that leaves us exactly twenty-five minutes to find a short enough queue to get into somewhere decent before we get locked out for the night."

I shrugged; there was no point in pursuing it.

Selfish bastard, I thought. "Lead on then," I said. Gerry gave me a sideways grin and without further discussion we both turned and began the walk that descended down Niddry Street, the steep crevasse of buildings which led to the lowest level in the old town: the Cowgate, our capital's night time party land.

3. Descent

In recent years, the Cowgate had become the place to be if music, drink and no dress code were your thing. If you wanted to hang with the impressively dressed spending wads of cash, you would head for the glitzy carnage of George Street and the New Town. If your thing was playing the shell suit lottery, you could throw on your finest casual sports gear and play good bar/ropey bar roulette in Lothian Road where the neds herded unpredictably. However, if you wanted occasionally decent music without too many contrived surroundings and fashion restrictions (but still with the overpriced beer), there was the younger network of venues which ran along the half mile or so between Bannerman's Bar in the Cowgate and the Salsa Bar in the Grassmarket.

But we were not the only people out looking for a late venue that night. As soon as we walked the first few yards down Niddry Street, we saw our first queue, a lengthy group of partygoers tailing up towards us from Binkies Bar's front door.

"Nah," said Gerry immediately, as he eyed up the long line of bodies. "That's just a live music pub anyway, not hardcore enough."

We squinted through the windows as we walked past and saw it was jam-packed. I liked the place. I had seen some good local bands there, but it was shoulder to shoulder inside, so I concurred. We walked further down Niddry Street until we had to step off the pavement on to the cobblestones because of the crowds outside the other bars. Finally, Gerry began to converse.

"Anyway Paul, you seem to be forgetting something about us these days."

"Like what?"

"Like, when you were on about things not being the way they used to be?"

"You *were* listening?"

"Yeah, 'course I was. But it's *never* going to be the same again, is it? We're what, at least a generation ahead of most of these folks? And we're both getting on a bit you know, even a bit wrinkly if I may be so bold. We started drinking round here about, when—seventeen, eighteen years ago? Longer maybe? We're just going to look like tired old gits to all these kids and students."

"Tired gits who are in the prime of their thirties if you don't mind?"

"Okay, grandpa. But, you know, when we were younger, everybody else was too. Guys our age now didn't even appear on our radar then, we would have been invisible. In our day we had our way with the ladies and everybody was our mate. Nowadays when we step into any of these places we probably just look like dads on the pull."

"It doesn't stop you trying to hump their legs though, does it?"

"Indeed," said Gerry. "But I have a serious responsibility there, you know. Every young girl needs a tale of heartbreak where some bad man sweeps her off her feet, promises her the world and then turns out to be an arsehole, leaving her in tatters. The way I see it, I don't mind being that terrible person their new boyfriends have to be better than. I'm providing a genuine service by setting the bar so low."

I gave him a dismayed look, but saw his 'I've-had-a-few-beers-and-no-one's-going-to-stop-me' grin.

"You're a twat," I said.

"Yeah, whatever, Mr Loverman," he drawled. "So where do you think we should be going then? A Bromide bar maybe? Church? The 'Jurassic'? That'll get your droop on for sure."

"I don't know," I said, "and also, don't care. But don't count on me hanging around till closing time—this guy here is not up for an all-nighter."

Gerry said nothing more. As we walked further down the steep, cobbled roadway I wondered if he was serious about the Jurassic. It was a common default for those who didn't make the city centre club curfew. Only a short and shameful taxi ride would take you out to the place we all knew as Jurassic Park, the old ballroom in the outskirts of Tollcross, which brazenly catered for the more 'mature' end of the nightlife market. Jesus, that was almost us...

A few seconds later we reached the bottom of Niddry Street, where the imposing stone buildings of the Cowgate rose up to their highest all around us. It was common knowledge, at least to anyone who had been on a guided tour there, that two or three hundred years ago, to save space and keep the city from growing beyond the city wall, the town planners (for want of a better term) did most of their new building either on top of any houses that could take the weight or atop any other existing foundations around at the time. Upwards instead of outwards, that was their vision.

It was also common knowledge that as a result of the constricted, ad-hoc building in the old town, there were still scores of known and unknown passages and recesses everywhere. Further up the High Street there were still entire unaltered streets of buildings preserved underground. Some had just become uninhabitable and obscured over the years whilst others were sealed off with plague victims still and ruthlessly forgotten, only to be turned into present day horror themed tourist traps.

But down in The Cowgate we were at level one, year zero (well, 1400-ish), and the streets didn't run any lower than that. This part of the city rose up in layers of thick-walled, vaulted stone warehouses accessed by open passages from the street, passages us locals call 'closes'. Even amidst the crowds and bright lights of weekend party time, it always seemed to me that the deeper you ventured down here, the more of the past you saw in the buildings. The walk down Niddry Street to The Cowgate always felt to me like some sort of architectural time travel.

However, the Cowgate was anything but forgotten. As we turned right at the foot of the street, we saw a bustling stretch of nightlife before us. From there on, we were constantly sidestepping and giving way to others, passing as we did, bar after club only to see queues of revellers outside that seemed to go on forever.

There was no problem finding somewhere to drink down there—the only problem at that time of night was getting past the licensing curfew imposed by the Council, the by-law that declared at 1:30 a.m. prompt, there was to be no more admission to any pubs or clubs, regardless of their closing time. No amount of pleading, bribing the doormen or shaming on Facebook would get you past the gatekeepers for that all important last hour or so. And that night it seemed as if everywhere was teeming with expectant hopefuls, constantly checking phones and watches to see how long they had left. We walked the entire length of the street and ended up being no further forward. Gerry looked at his own watch and scowled.

"Fuck," he said, "Ten more minutes left to get in somewhere."

I stayed silent but my urge to escape was growing. I was already at my time limit but I knew if I could ride out these last few minutes then I still stood a chance of making it home in time for some sleep before work and minimal earache from Gerry.

Our route took us past the last cluster of drinking dens on the south of the street then under the dark archway of George IV Bridge. We stopped on the pavement opposite the off-street walkway which led off road towards Shady Lady's Bar.

"Hey, there's not much of a queue outside Lady's," said Gerry, excitedly.

"I'm not surprised," I said, "That's a total last resort; last time I was in there it was full of daft wee laddies wanting to prove something."

Lady's was a place I had never been fond of. I had a bad experience there once, admittedly it had been years ago, but that once was enough. It had been one of those pointless face offs that everyone dreads in places like that. From what I remember, I had been out with friends and was unintentionally served ahead of some of them at the bar at one point. Or something. I knew something was up as I seemed to be getting glared at afterwards.

At a point later in the night, I left my own company to go to the bathroom, only to find a bunch of them waiting there for me, all of them bristling with testosterone and most likely, cheap coke. I was then given the whole 'what are you looking at?' routine from the smallest, mouthiest one—basically the prelude to being attacked.

Long story short, that had not been a situation I was going to get out of unharmed, so my hand was forced (so to speak).

Without any further discussion, I picked out the biggest one, lunged and put him down decisively, which scattered the rest in the process. Thankfully, the surprise element worked and no follow up attack was offered. As it turned out, the display had the desired effect, they all backed off, suddenly unsure of what they were dealing with, whilst I turned around and walked. No injuries other than the big man's pride, me feeling like a twat for having to do it, and of course my poor expanded bladder, as I never did get to the bathroom.

Don't get me wrong, that's no war story and I'm no action movie hardass, but sometimes you have to make an assessment out of context to your situation and act on it. Had it been some dive bar in Kabul, then it just would have been another day at work—but it's shit when some idiots ruin your night like that in a safe and civilised Scottish bar. So yes, Shady's may well have changed since then, but as far as I was concerned, a club lives or dies on its first impressions, and that place was not my idea of a good time bar.

"Come *onnnn*. It's a place to go. It's beer and music, man," said Gerry as he began to stride off towards the end of the short queue. I paused and thought about protesting further—but then walked wearily after him, assessing by the time that I would most likely never see the inside.

As we joined the line, I checked my watch. It was a couple of minutes before half past one and there were still at least half a dozen bodies ahead of us. There seemed a very high probability we wouldn't make it in. But even then, I could feel my stomach beginning to knot. For some reason I had a very bad feeling in my gut, something I couldn't quite explain, a discomfort that felt deeper than just the fear of a hangover and potentially falling out with the neds inside.

Then, just as that magic minute was upon us, the doors opened to release a deluge of noise, light and drunken partygoers. They laughed, shouted and sang tunelessly, dancing obliviously past us towards the main road and the chance of a taxi. Their night was probably over now—lucky them.

Two men by the doors caught my eye. A couple of security guys wearing black flying jackets with "Lady's Niteclub" embroidered on the front began to wave the people directly in front of us into the club. By this time a few more bodies had drifted into the line behind us, most likely as hard up for a beer as we were.

My watch now said 01:32; I said nothing.

Another minute or so passed before the larger of the two doormen, a hulk of a guy physically blocking the doorway with his frame looked at his watch. He silently nodded to the other; a small, wiry looking guy with lank, fine hair and a drooping moustache which may or may not have been ironic. The smaller guy seemed to be in charge as he had the clicker in his hand for counting people in and out. His face was set in a scowl and his whole demeanour read, 'wee man/big chip on shoulder: avoid.'

"Okay, folks!" barked wee man. "It's past that time and there's no one else getting in here now. Move off home right away please!" I heard mutters of discontent behind us and turned to walk off back to the Cowgate along with the rest of the unsuccessfuls, working out how best to disguise my relief that our night had harmlessly come to a natural end.

"Well, I guess that's it," I said to Gerry as I turned, "Come on, I reckon that rain will be on soon anyway..."

But it was his pissed off alter-ego that replied.

"What? No fucking way—they can't do that to us!" he said, slowly shaking his head. I sighed, this was not a good sign. Gerry, for all he was a good mate, he also had previous for being a liability with a few drinks in him and, whilst he was never one to start any trouble, as long as his evil twin was in charge he would never walk away from any either. I tried my best to sound diplomatic, "They just did. Look, you know the way it works with these guys," I said. "They've got a little bit of power here and they'll make a big deal about using it—now back off."

"What? No way!" Gerry argued, "I counted eight people coming out there a minute ago—those bastards only let six in."

"Gerry, leave it, there's no point, remember the kind of guys you're dealing with here, it's not worth it..."

But there was no stopping him, "Don't worry, I'll be polite," he said. Which usually meant trouble.

"Hey, guys!" he was shouting at the doormen now, "There were eight bodies came out of there a minute ago, you only let six in—that's hardly fair!"

"Sorry, mate," hissed the smaller doorman, "We're just doin' a job here. Now do us a favour and piss off somewhere else."

With that he stepped forward into brighter light and I got a better look at him. Again, I was getting that whole 'reduced stature/nervous aggression' vibe off him which was probably helping stoke the bad feeling in my gut. I also saw he had a name-badge on his jacket just under the club logo; his name was Norman. Norman the doorman, Jesus, give me a break.

4. Confrontation

But Gerry wasn't about to see the amusing side.

"That is fucking ridiculous," he continued, "even you plums must be able to count to eight? They had to come out in single file to get past us. I watched you count them out on the clicker!"

Norman shrugged, pocketed his clicker and said nothing—but I saw the smile under his moustache, he was enjoying the confrontation and his power over it.

"Maybe we can count—but didn't let you in 'cos we just don't like whingin' arseholes," the bigger one laughed. He also stepped into the light and I saw his name-badge simply said 'Al'. I didn't need to overthink things to see this was a flashpoint situation. Where I tended to ignore most doormen if they started the el cheapo hard man routine, I knew that right now Gerry would only see it as a blistering red rag to a bull.

"It could also be because you're just a couple of useless fucking dickheads who can't count the number of fingers on one hand?" ranted Gerry. Okay, shots fired on both sides now but still manageable. This wasn't like the drama I'd had in the club before, I just needed to get him out of there before anything developed. I stepped over to Gerry and put my arm around him in a 'come on, you old drunken mate, you,' sort of way and began to guide him around.

"Leave it Gerry, this won't get us anywhere," I said. He quickly shrugged me off. I saw Norman was bristling at this exchange. He was now turning around to speak into his hand-held radio. I also saw his larger colleague clearly fumbling for something under his jacket the way someone might reach for a weapon. Surely that was just a bluff for show?

Gerry continued his 'reasoning', oblivious to what was going on around him.

"So, what do you say? You let us in and we'll all be friends or I take your incompetence with numbers up with your supervisors?"

"I know," snarled Al, "Why don't you just go away and fuck yourself in the empty head?" It was all pretty puerile stuff, but I could tell it was sending Gerry ballistic. That was enough. I moved forward again and reached out to grab Gerry by the arm; unconditional retreat was clearly the safest option for everyone now. But Gerry stepped forward out of reach before I could grab him and mouthed off some more.

"What the fuck d'you think...?"

But he stopped dead as Al suddenly pulled out a short, black baton from the fold of his jacket. He slapped it down hard in his hand for effect and walked menacingly towards Gerry. Behind him Norman still cradled his radio, his voice now rising in pitch, demanding that whoever was at the other end should, 'send the crew down to hand these tossers their arses,' or similar. As always, I was surprised at how little time it had taken for such a bad situation to have grown from absolutely nothing.

With hindsight of course, this was the point where both of us should have abandoned all self-esteem and ran. I still remember standing there weighing up possible outcomes like a kid watching a fight about to kick off in the playground. Comparing Gerry to Big Al, if it came down to size alone it might look like a fair match, but what that muscle-bound sentry wouldn't know was, unlike a lot of other pure weight grunters, Gerry backed up his bulk with aerobic exercise, mostly by way of hitting things: MMA, BJJ and boxing at least. If you asked him, the list would probably go on until it sent you to sleep; it was one of his coping mechanisms.

My own guts were still leaden with the overpowering sense of risk, not of losing any potential fight but of winning it—and then having to explain to the law and the suits afterwards how infantile and unnecessary it had all been. I turned and tried to make a show of walking away, hoping Gerry would just snap out of it.

"Come on mate, you know these guys aren't worth it, get your arse over here now!" I shouted with a bit of tone, hoping it might spark off some of the old discipline in him, praying he would snap out of it before we came to blows between ourselves. But no, he seemed fixated.

"And who the fuck do you think you're going to intimidate with that thing?" Gerry mocked, standing his ground whilst Al, like a prize twat, made a threateningly slow approach towards him, probably expecting Gerry to bottle it and run.

And so it began. Those next few moments which changed everyone's lives forever felt like an eternity, yet they were over in a flash. But I suppose that's the way it is with most fights, regardless of the outcome.

Without a further word spoken, Big Al accelerated as he closed in on Gerry, raising his baton in a high, kinetic arc over his last couple of paces. I saw the baton swing down towards Gerry's face—but Gerry smoothly drew his hands out of his pockets, raised his arm and easily blocked the blow. Barely a heartbeat passed before a counter punch was delivered straight to the doorman's face. As the blow connected I heard the crunch of cartilage and saw an almost instant flow of blood from his nose.

This sudden violence grabbed Norman's attention. He turned from his radio to look over at the three of us. Now that physical blows had been traded he was clearly out of his depth; his expression a giveaway of stark horror.

Al reeled from the blow. He threw his free hand up to his face then pulled it away almost immediately looking strangely surprised to see the mess of red, wet matter in his palm. He looked at Gerry with a glare that said, 'I'm going to kill you for that,' and growled like an angered animal. Al then lunged with all his considerable weight, but was neatly sidestepped by Gerry, who saw him coming a mile off.

As Al passed him harmlessly by, Gerry spun with him, dropping his hand down firmly to the back of Al's shaven head, guiding him skilfully downwards as he passed through the empty space where, a fraction of a second earlier, Gerry had stood.

Al was now in a critical position, off balance and lumbering. As I knew he would, Gerry moved in to end the confrontation with minimal effort as his leg hooked out one of Al's stumbling feet, sending him off balance and down towards the ground where he landed with an ungracious thud.

Gerry stood where he was, shaking his head, looking at the sprawled doorman and probably thinking of some Hollywood style one liner to finish the moment. But I checked his back and saw Norman had suddenly sprang into action. He was fast, I hadn't expected that, and I was surprised he'd found the bottle to get involved on a physical level. But then as he moved in, I saw what was giving him the confidence as I caught a flash of metal in his hand which glinted in the streetlight.

In that split second, I realised he had pulled a knife and was about to bury it in Gerry's back. I don't even remember shouting a warning as I launched past a bewildered Gerry and grabbed a hold of the knife-wielding arm of Norman.

Thankfully he wasn't particularly solid, and I managed to stop him short before he found his mark. He yelped as I squeezed hard into his wrist, trying to twist the blade around and out of his grip. He was stronger and wirier than I'd expected though, and straight away he started thrashing himself around and taking me with him.

Despite his diminutive size, I felt as if I properly had my hands full with him. I yelled at him to drop the blade, probably more for the benefit of anyone who might have been watching (or worse, filming), and missed that I was acting defensively.

But now he was too far gone. Despite my best efforts he caught me out with his other hand and planted me square on the face. Bastard. Straight away I felt blood running in my own nose and down the back of my throat. I shook my head to clear the shock whilst still keeping his knife hand at a distance—there was no way I was letting go of this guy now.

"Fuck's sake!" I heard Gerry gasp behind me as he caught up with events. Next thing I knew, Gerry skipped forward and planted a side kick in Norman's stomach, knocking the breath and the fight right out of him. As he doubled up I held on tight to his arm then gave it a hard twist which caused him to keel over and drop the blade on the ground, where it bounced and clattered away behind us along the walkway.

With Norman also down, Gerry and I exchanged looks of disbelief. This couldn't really be happening to us, could it? I wiped the blood away from my upper lip. My nose was throbbing but I'd had worse, although not whilst out for a quiet drink in town.

Then, in what must have been the very next second, I saw Gerry's eyes draw to a point behind me. I anticipated what was coming next and ducked as Gerry lunged past me towards the spot where Big Al had fallen. I whipped round to see Gerry fully launch himself at Al, who had obviously recovered from his takedown quicker than expected and was back on his feet, the discarded knife now held tight in both hands. He had clearly lost the plot and now intended to do some real harm.

Gerry swept his arms heavily to the side and grabbed him—in a heartbeat their bodies became tightly locked together, each struggling viciously, a tangle of limbs with the occasional flash of dangerous metal in the mix.

I quickly stepped over and tried to intervene, to free the knife for a second time. I gripped one of Al's arms with all my strength, but he hauled away using his weight as a lever, throwing me off balance.

Still with my hands locked around his arm, he spun and all of us toppled down towards the ground. As I pushed my arms out to break my fall, Al then viciously snatched his own arm back into the rolling struggle.

But as the heavy mass of bone and body rolled over on the cobblestones, there was a stark, tearing sound followed by a prolonged murmur and the watery hiss of escaping breath. I froze—I knew that sound. As I looked on, I saw Al roll on to his back and a pool of thick, dark liquid begin to spread out from underneath the tangled bodies.

For a few seconds both bodies lay deathly still. Then, as if some kind of sudden realisation had struck him, Gerry pushed himself up quickly to reveal the wooden handle of the knife protruding awkwardly out from Al's chest. There was an obvious line of blood streaked right across the front of Gerry's shirt.

Despite all our training and everything we had lived through and learned in combat, a moment of panic sparked between us.

"No. Fuck no. No way..." gasped Gerry, "What the fuck are we going to do now?"

I couldn't speak, my own mind was also racing.

This was the worst of worst-case scenarios.

Just then, as we stood there in that moment of disbelief, the twin doors of the nightclub rattled as they burst open, and five burly figures emerged from the pulsating light and noise beyond. All were dressed in the same black flying jackets as the first two, each one appeared to be just as physically formidable as big Al, as their silhouettes blocked out any view beyond the doorframe.

Gerry turned his head towards the approaching group, and I saw his fists clench—he was going to go for it. I gripped his arm hard—that time I got his attention; I had my answer.

"I think we're going to run," I said.

5. Run

We set off at a sprint making our way back towards the Cowgate, knowing that the best place to shake them off would be the network of passageways and closes there. As we reached the main street we began dodging and weaving around taxis and drunken bodies, spurred on by the threats and screams of our pursuers, who hadn't wasted any time in giving chase. From what I could hear there was no point in either of us running as we were both dead men already.

Faces and cars flashed by as startled pedestrians swore at us and pissed off car drivers blasted their horns in our wake. We stopped at nothing, sprinting as fast as we could, trying to keep a decent amount of space between us and the mob.

By the time we reached the close which separated the converted church-come-nightclub, Wilkie House and the Kitchen Bar next door, we had managed to put a fair bit of distance between them and us. I was just thankful those meathead types usually ran out of breath pretty quickly.

Gerry and I scrambled around the corner almost losing our footing at the speed we took the turn. Inside the narrow, dimly lit close we straightened ourselves up and slowed to a fast walk. We both knew this was a good call as this passage led further into the bowels of the Old Town and there was more than one way out—it gave us options.

"Should we split up?" Gerry asked on an exhale.

"Too dangerous," I said, "they're really pissed off. If they caught either of us on our own we would never stand a chance." He knew I was right.

"Better lose them then," he said, and at that I heard the threatening screams grow nearer as if they were approaching the entrance to the close. I had hoped we might have slipped their line of vision in the crowd as we made the turn, but then I didn't want to stop at the time to judge the distance. Both of us bolted onwards up the inclined path and steep stairway which led past La Belle Angele, until we took a further turn and emerged at the top of the climb amongst the high tenement flats of Guthrie Street.

Again, we slowed to match the speed of the walking crowd. This street was pretty much student residential, lined with newish university flats built after a gas explosion had levelled half of the original street years before. Student flats on a Friday night meant lots of late-night activity, so there were more bodies there milling around making it easier to mingle and blend.

"Where to now?" Gerry asked, the bastard was hardly even out of breath. I found myself wishing I'd kept my fitness up the same way he had over the years. I glanced around—we could have run south into Chambers Street but that was a wide-open road blocked along one side by the Museum—no place to hide if we were spotted. We could have tried one of the other closes and hid ourselves until later—but that wouldn't be tolerable, plus there was far too high a risk of them getting lucky.

"Back down," I gasped.

"What?"

"Back down to the Cowgate—under the arches at the court building and up the next close on the left,"

"We just came that way!"

"Just do it..." I barked; there was no time for persuasion now, he had to be ordered.

Gerry said nothing more and followed on. If I was right, the mob would follow us through the close we had just left, then assume we would keep moving further away once we reached the far end. My plan was to take us back on ourselves, but if we ran downwards in Guthrie Street we would emerge on the Cowgate further back from where we had turned off, behind our pursuers. We set off at a run and a glance behind told me we would be around the corner and out of sight before the mob reached the top of the steps at the back of us—they wouldn't know for sure which way we had gone.

Within seconds we were back down in the busy Cowgate, jogging lightly along the stretch of pavement towards the cover of the thick foundation pillars under the court buildings above. Now it was only the occasional homebound partygoer giving us any sort of passing looks, so we slowed and stopped beside a row of piss-soaked waste bins there.

I chanced another look behind us—there was nothing obvious I could see. We were now standing at the foot of another narrow, high sided close which led away from the Cowgate into the cover of another parallel side-street beyond. We began the brisk walk up the passageway, doing our best to avoid the fresh pooling of urine on the steps. As we neared the top I saw the black and gold street sign fixed on the wall high above the summit: 'Dyer's Close,' it said—how appropriate.

At the top of the steps we stilled ourselves as best we could to listen for any sound of pursuit. There was still a drunken cacophony from the far end of the close mixed with distant screams which may or may not have been the masses still enjoying the good times beyond. We lingered a few seconds and listened to the drifting voices exaggerated by the echo off the high stone walls—but the screams became more and more indistinct.

If the plan had worked, our pursuers would have assumed we had taken the more obvious escape route from Guthrie Street to elsewhere in town, and with a bit of luck they would now be searching amongst the wine and jazz bars of the Southside. With a bit more luck, they might just have made a few wrong turnings and ended up completely lost—it was easy done if you didn't know the rat runs. For the first time I found myself quietly thanking those bygone town planners for the infuriating layout of this part of the city.

We were now in the next street up, Merchant Street, a cul-de-sac with one end blanked on our left by the imposing 'customer' entrance to the Sheriff Court. On our right, the roadway led to another narrow one-way street between Greyfriars Churchyard and the Cowgatehead below. Our street felt oppressive, dominated and darkened as it was by a massive low stone archway, the underside of a road bridge above which spanned across one side of the street to the other. It was effectively a dark stone canopy which, at its lowest parts, had just enough headroom to allow pedestrians to clear it whilst walking underneath.

Conscious of the CCTV cameras peering our way from the court entrance, we walked away from them as casually as we could to a point under the wide arch, where we stopped to catch our breath. I felt my chest heaving with the unexpected effort and shock of it all—but it seemed, in that moment at least, we were safe.

"Christ..." I gasped. I found it hard to put the racing thoughts into words.

"I..." Gerry gasped, the exertion finally catching up with him, "...didn't mean to..." He looked numb. He shook his head, "*Jesus*—it wasn't my *fault*..."

But it really was, and he knew it.

"That guy looked as if he could be finished back there," I said. Gerry responded by looking morose and clasping his hands behind his head, pulling it down from behind to stare at the pavement.

"You know what we should do?" I spluttered. I wasn't entirely sure if I knew myself or if I was asking Gerry. There was a pause punctuated by our breathing and the sound of my own heart pounding in my ears. Then, as he often did, Gerry offered a late reply, "Yes. Yes, I know what we should do—we should be sensible. Go to the police and tell them what really happened. We should go through all that 'our side of the story' crap."

Even after all of that he could still manage enough sarcasm to make me want to kick that 'bad fuckin' attitude' all the way out of him and off down the street. I somehow got the impression that despite everything he still wasn't prepared to redeem himself like an adult. I felt my temper fraying further,

"*Yes!*" I was shouting by then, "You're right, we *will* go to the police—and we *will* tell them what happened, right down to the last detail! There's no way I'm going to be running away like some criminal because some macho fuckwit doesn't know when to go home!"

Gerry shook his head slowly but kept his eyes fixed straight down. He knew I meant what I said and he knew I was right. Also, we both knew it would never be that simple.

"So, we explain it to the cops," I said, "and then, as soon as our names flag on their intelligence systems, the spooks from our old job will know—and then we'll also have to try and explain this whole sorry clusterfuck to them." I looked over at Gerry whose head seemed to bow even lower at the thought.

I turned and slammed my fist hard into the wall. Frustration, anger, fear—everything was now fogging my head, wooling up my thoughts, stopping me from thinking clearly. I was also picturing the wall being Gerry's head at that moment—but we were past fighting among ourselves, that would only draw even more unwanted attention. In the worst possible way, it seemed to be just like the old days, we had to work as a team if we were going to get out of there safely. The pain in my staved hand helped as a throbbing reminder not to start losing it.

I began to pace the cobblestones while Gerry continued staring downwards, trance-like. I worked on getting my thoughts into some kind of order as my breathing and heartbeat slowed down. I became aware of the night air feeling cool through my shirt and jacket. I took some deep, measured breaths—keep the head—be logical, you twat.

"Alright," I said eventually. "Alright. Okay, it *was* an accident. You might have been behaving like a fucking two-year-old!" I felt the anger rise again as the words came out—I raised my hands—no, calm down, start again. "...but it *was* unintentional," I said, "It really was. I know it was. The little guy pulled a blade, I disarmed him, the big guy then came at you with a blade, I saw it happen. He looked as if he'd lost the plot, as if he was really going to use it—you responded by using necessary force." The familiar phrase from our past stung us both. Gerry slid to his haunches and cupped his hands around his face. He gave out a deep sigh from behind them.

"Jesus!" I took another deep breath and looked up at the underside of the archway above, pacing a few steps out on to the road. How the hell were we going to get out of this one?

But when my gaze returned to street level, my heart missed a beat. Two girls had been watching us from the pavement at the edge of the bridge, obviously listening to everything.

6. Haven

They were standing silently in the shadow of the arch maybe fifteen feet or so away, smoking cigarettes and leaning casually against the iron railings which separated the pavement from the tenements. The stone canopy intensified all the sound under it, I knew our voices must have carried. Had they been there all along? Probably. Shit.

"You boys in some kind of trouble?" asked the smaller of the two. I lifted my hand up to filter out the glare of the streetlight behind them and saw she was a slender girl with pale skin and layered blonde hair which hung loosely around her shoulders. Her silhouette outlined a slight but well-defined figure in what looked like some sort of dark one-piece catsuit. Maybe not the most practical eveningwear, but her poise was so casual and confident that somehow it looked just right on her. Besides, who was I kidding—dressing like that would barely even register around the Old Town clubs on a Friday night. Her eyes were narrowed, as if examining me, assessing us.

So—what to say when lost for words. Blurting out the whole sorry story would be stupid but it would have felt good to offload to someone right then, to share the problem further. The conflict must have lit me up like a beacon as I began to stammer, looking for something to say that wouldn't sound like a lie.

"No," I said—although it may well have been, "Yes."

Both girls turned to one another and whispered amongst themselves. The second girl, who was taller, bending forwards slightly to hear the blonde girl's words. It seemed as if there was some sort of hurried debate going on. I didn't like it—it felt as if I had been put on hold while they conferred.

As my eyes adjusted to the backlight I began to see more detail. The blonde girl was young—they were both young—possibly early to mid-twenties, but there the likeness ended. The taller girl was just short of my own height with a mane of long, black hair and a severe fringe which accentuated her high cheekbones. She looked lean and was dressed more plainly in what looked like a man's white shirt and worn, black leather trousers. Her arms were folded in front of her as the conferring continued, the tip of her cigarette dancing with her movement and glowing, held at just the right angle to let the smoke drift away from her clothes. There was no denying both these girls were attractive—but they also looked capable, as if they could probably handle themselves in a fight.

I suddenly became aware I was paying them far more attention than I should be. Daft wee lassies looking for a bit of chat and drama—maybe some other time. I paced back over to the crumpled form of Gerry, still with his head in his hands. I kicked him gently as a prompt to pull him out of his fit of woe. When I looked back up, I saw both girls scrutinising him. After a second or two, both glanced at each other and nodded almost imperceptibly, a movement so subtle I surely would have missed it had I not been so strung out.

The blonde one spoke again, "I'm just wondering, do either of you happen to have mobile telephones with you?"

Seemed an odd question.

"Funny you should ask—but no," I said. Another glance and a slight nod passed between the girls, and the dark-haired girl smiled, as if that was just what she wanted to hear.

"It's just, well, you won't get any reception under that bridge there," she added.

Bit of a puzzling introduction, I thought.

"Okay, thanks for that. Where did you two spring from, anyway?" I asked, trying conspicuously to hold my voice steady.

Gerry looked up to see who I was speaking to, and as I suspected he might, he quickly began to push himself upwards in an effort to regain some credibility in light of our sudden female company.

"Hmm," said the dark-haired girl, "We just came up for some air, it's just a wee bit stuffy down in the club."

"What club?" I asked, dreading that the answer might be Lady's, even though that was a street away.

"Medusa," she replied quietly, nodding back over her shoulder past the railings. I assumed there were probably some recessed steps behind her leading to some place below street level. That wasn't unusual, a lot of bars and shops in the Old Town were accessed the same way—but I couldn't recall ever having seen one there before. I stepped forward to take a look, and as I moved closer I realised there was muffled music coming from somewhere beyond them—something was obviously going on down there after all. I heard Gerry shuffle up behind me.

"I've never heard of that one," he croaked.

"No, you wouldn't have. We don't advertise," said the dark-haired girl.

I turned to Gerry—this was wasting time, we needed to be away from there, and fast. He shot me a look that asked 'what are we going to do with this?'

"Well, it looks like you're in trouble to me," the blonde girl said, with a gentle barb of insistence. She nodded towards Gerry's bloodstained shirt which I realised then looked very obvious close up. Gerry folded his arms as if this would make the mess disappear, and he began to stammer something which was cut short.

"Oh, you're hurt too," the taller girl directed at me. In a swift movement which took me by surprise, she quickly stepped forward and reached out, wiping some of the blood spatter off my shirt with a handkerchief she must have had balled in her non-smoking fist. In the earlier chase I had forgotten all about my own injury.

"Err... thank you," I said. She smiled, clutched the handkerchief, then stepped nimbly backwards to her friend, quickly folding her arms again.

"I'm Keisha," said the blonde girl. "This is my best friend, Teagan."

"We do *everything* together," said Teagan with a mischievous smile. She knew it was a cockteasing cliché and I wondered if she meant it as a joke. Keisha chuckled at her friend's remark, took a final draw on her cigarette and threw it down on the pavement, stubbing it out under the toe of a black Doc Marten boot.

"Maybe you would both like to come down and join the party?" she asked.

"What about the curfew?" asked Gerry.

"We don't have a curfew, it's a private party. No licence, nothing to do with the Council—or anyone else here," said Teagan. "Don't worry though, we have all our permissions, it's all legal, we just run it as a sort of... co-operative."

I turned to Gerry and nodded silently. Yes, it was a plan—a place to go to get us out of sight in the meantime. He quickly nodded, he understood. But the exchange was broken by the sound of shouting behind us.

"Look! That's them there—pair of baa*staards*!" I turned to see two of our earlier pursuers emerging a short distance away from the top of the stairway at Dyer's Close. In a heartbeat they quickened their pace, making their way towards us. I saw both had weapons in their hands not unlike Al's baton from earlier.

"Come ahead—you *fuuucks!*" the biggest one bellowed with as much venom as he might have had left in him. He broke into a lumbering run and I saw in his face he was intent on nothing but hurt. Both girls seemed strangely unfazed by this—but we were going to have to do something, and fast.

"Okay. Maybe you two would be *safer* if you came downstairs with us," said Keisha, with a disturbing air of calm.

"I think so," I said quickly. At this, both girls turned and nimbly fled down a steep set of steps which led from the pavement to a sturdy looking door in the tenement building below street level. Gerry and I hastily followed and watched as Keisha gave a series of knocks on the door which were obviously coded. Bizarre.

As seconds passed I noticed there was a white mask hung on the wall adjacent to the door, similar to a masquerade disguise with messy, red lines striped across the face just around and below the eyes. Maybe it was the clubland equivalent of putting balloons up outside a house where the party was. My heart began to pound as I heard the footfall of approaching thugs echo in the archway above.

But within the space of a few heartbeats, the door swung open and we were quickly ushered inside. I was last to step through the door, and as I did so I felt it swing heavily closed. Metal scraped on metal as a large iron bar slid coarsely across the door's rear, locking it solidly into place. Our pursuers must have been right behind us—but where I expected to hear banging on the door as soon as it was closed, I heard nothing. Maybe they had decided to keep 'eyes on' and were calling reinforcements? Yes, probably that.

Once inside, I saw we were in a reception room of sorts. The lighting was strange there, ultraviolet strips hung suspended overhead with strings of cheap-looking fairy lights pinned around the walls. There was enough light to see by, but the shapes inside that didn't highlight under the ultraviolets were gloomy and odd. Immediately behind the door was a solid wooden desk which had seen better times, and some old-looking wooden chairs. Some out of date notice boards lay at odd angles around the walls and on the main wall above the desk there was a crisply unfolded map of the world with a number of pins stuck in it, seemingly at random.

Ahead of us were twin doors with oval windows which pulsated with lights from beyond—probably the main part of the club. In all, it looked to me as if we were standing in some old, disused disco bar that had hastily been put back into service.

"Don't worry," said Teagan to Gerry.

"You'll be safe with us," said Keisha to me.

"Just wait a minute." A man stepped out of the shadows behind the doorway; this must have been the guy who opened the door for us.

"Who said you two could come in here?" He was looking directly at us, his eyes narrowed in a malevolent stare. This doorman was different from the usual crew, he wasn't particularly bulky or tall, but the neat cut of his black suit and dead looking eyes gave him a sense of subtle menace. This man was no boneheaded thug; he had the air of being truly dangerous.

Keisha spoke for us, "It's okay Vincent, we've invited them in as special guests."

Teagan then drew up close to his ear and pursed her lips as she quietly whispered the words, "*Cochon longues...*" Some kind of password? I wasn't sure if I was supposed to have heard or not— maybe the words went along with the coded knocks. The doorman nodded slowly, tolerantly, his steely expression didn't falter, his eyes never leaving mine.

"Just don't cause any trouble," he said to us slowly. "We don't do trouble here."

Normally this would have had my back right up, but all Gerry and I could do was nod compliantly. It was clear this guy didn't negotiate, and with the wrecking crew undoubtedly gathering outside, these people were now holding all of our cards. I was the one to break his stare by looking over at the bolted door. If anything, at least it looked more than capable of keeping the lynch mob out for the moment.

"Come on, guys," said Keisha as she walked off. We turned and followed as they led us over to the double doors where the coloured lights pulsed through the glass. Above them I saw a sign crudely painted above the doors glowing neon green in the ultra violet, it said: 'Club Medusa - Enjoy.'

I knew it was wrong, but I couldn't help but admire the backlit figures of both girls as they slinked through the doors and turned to hold them open for us. An old Grandmaster Flash track was playing inside, the bass rumble took me right back to my younger days, probably the last time I had heard it. Strangely, Gerry and I both paused there as if something were holding us back. I glanced round and saw he was giving me a look. I could read him—he thought something wasn't sitting right with it all. I knew, because I felt it too.

"Gentlemen, please?" said Teagan, gesturing us to enter. But we knew we were committed, the only way to go now was forward. We walked through the doors into the music and took in the view.

*

The layout of the sprawling cavern inside wasn't unusual for this part of the Old Town. It was a low room annexed by a series of interconnecting stone vaulted chambers and alcoves. The central part of the club with the dancefloor was easily seen from the entrance doors, but beyond that the room was broken into sections divided by stone pillars which formed a series of open archways surrounding the central part of the club.

Although it looked as if the place was probably a good size, very little could be seen from any one viewpoint without peering around pillars or walking into alcoves. Low lit passages led off from the main part of the room in all directions while stone recesses seemed all around, asymmetrical and darkened. It was gothic alright, but then virtually every other pub, club and shop at this level of the city was much the same, most choosing to make the vaulted cellar look a feature rather than spending a fortune renovating.

In the centre of the room were a few bodies dancing on to the thump of the bass on a large and new-looking temporary wooden dance floor. On our right was a crudely lit mobile disco enclosure where the huddled figure of a DJ fidgeted in the lamplight with an arrangement of decks and mixers. Teagan broke off from us and immediately made a beeline for him.

At the farthest side of the dance floor was a well-lit table on which lay the remains of a large buffet, leftover food scattering its surface like scraps left at the end of a hungry wedding. Arranged randomly around the room were seats of all different types and sizes; some looked as if they were built into the walls but there were also odd-looking sofas and wooden chairs arranged around a motley collection of different styled tables. Nothing matched, it all looked begged, stolen or borrowed. And as if that wasn't enough, the patrons appeared every bit as odd and varied as their surroundings. It was difficult to make out the fine detail through the strobes, but there seemed to be almost every size, shape, age and gender imaginable in the place. From nimble-looking pensioners to middle aged, conservatively dressed parent types, elder and bat goths to young trendies, academic sorts and young girls like Keisha and Teagan—it was oddly surreal. As I scanned around further, I couldn't help but notice that regardless of all the diversity, everyone seemed to be effortlessly mingling, seemingly engaged in cheerful conversation.

Gerry nudged me. "This place is beginning to ring a bell for me," he said. "I'm sure I ended up in here at the end of a session a couple of years ago, not long after—you know, one of the things we don't mention. I was pretty out of it—I don't remember much—just that this was some late-night dive that no one ever came to unless everywhere else was closed."

"What was it like back then? I don't suppose you remember the ways in and out?" I asked.

"Looked pretty much the same as this from what I remember, a bit of a dive. I don't remember coming in the way we did, but as I said, I was gashed. I think the entrance was a bit further down the main road. I don't think the place was open for long, went bankrupt I think. Looks like somebody got hold of the licence and opened it back up. Obviously at no expense..."

My eyes were drawn to a group of four or five Latino girls on the dance floor, trying to speak to each other over the strains of the music. Then, almost as if we were the point of discussion, they turned to us, smiled and waved as if they knew us. I waved back awkwardly and swiftly turned away, feeling my face burn as if I'd been caught looking.

I began to do what I should have been doing—scanning for potential escape routes. Nothing seemed obvious. There was a bar to our left, it seemed a spartan affair with a few makeshift optics stands and mismatched mirrors propped up against the wall like afterthoughts. Below the line of their reflections were wine bottles arranged in rows along the back wall. Strangely there was no one standing there propping up the bar and no obvious bar staff waiting to serve either. My attention was drawn back to the outline of Teagan as she weaved her way back towards us across the dance floor.

"And if you ever decide to stop gawking and get us some drinks, we'll have two medium bodied chardonnays, please," said Keisha, which made me realise I'd been staring again. I turned around to see Gerry was already moving across the dancefloor, heading in the direction of the bar.

"Sure, of course—two medium bodied, err—chardonnays," I repeated, hoping it would stick with me.

"We're just going to the bathroom," said Teagan. With that, both walked off over part of the dancefloor and then in towards a recess on the left, chatting as they went. I couldn't hear a thing either of them were saying over the music.

I joined Gerry at the bar. When I got there, I shot another quick glance back at the girls and saw Teagan holding something up to her nose and mouth. For just a fraction of a second, she turned and glanced over at me—then quickly turned away. I could have sworn she was nuzzling that bloodied handkerchief from earlier. No, that would be gross. She was probably just itching her nose. Get real.

7. Paranoid

The bar seemed minimal to say the least. I scanned the line of optics, most of which were crudely nailed to a wooden plinth above the bar and saw there wasn't much choice. A bottle or two of Chartreuse, an almost empty bottle of Absinthe, some ports and sherries were there but the usual suspects such as whiskey, vodka, rums and gins were all noticeably absent.

I couldn't see any beer taps so I guessed they must have sold it bottled. They did have wine though; I could see some bottles were uncorked and lined up against the back of the bar. There were even more sitting in segmented cardboard boxes stacked against the rear wall. From the pale greens and clear glass of the bottles I guessed whites were popular. Just as well.

"They want white wines," I said to Gerry, who was already holding a £20 note up in full view to attract the attention of the absent bar staff. Fair enough, this didn't look like the kind of place that used card readers. He nodded and lowered his money; we were obviously going to have to wait.

"Well, what do you think?" he said, as he turned and scanned around.

"I think the lynch mob will still be outside and we're still screwed."

"No, about this place?"

I turned again and took in the scene. It still seemed odd, the mismatch and merging of furniture and generations. It really did look like a hurriedly organised gathering of some strange family.

"I don't like it," I said, "It's all a bit weird for me. I mean, I'm bloody glad we got in here when we did, but something about this place isn't sitting right."

"Oh, come on ya naysayer," said Gerry, obviously wanting to believe.

I shrugged, there was no point in dressing things up to make him feel better.

"Look Gerry, we're in a tight spot as it is—the last thing we need right now is any more grief. It all seems a bit convenient to me, those girls had no reason to invite us in, did they?"

"Yeah they did—they saw we were in the shit, so they did the right thing and helped us out."

"Maybe. Or maybe it was them that got lucky? They saw we were in the shit and all out of options? For all we know this could be some kind of honey trap setting us up for a massive taxing when we try to leave. You know about all those scams in the Soho clubs, right?"

He nodded, "Jesus Paul, yes, I know about them. I'm just trying to be positive here. Look, you saw the cut of the door on this place, and you must have got the vibe from that guy working it—I doubt anyone will be getting in here that they don't want in. I reckon we were lucky to get in ourselves. And all these people, they seem, well—they seem kind of normal; there are grandmothers here for fuck's sake! I'm getting a weird vibe too but no—there's no way this is some London bait club setup, and so far, I'm not picking up on any threats. I think we'll be safe enough here for a bit, at least until things cool down outside, right?"

I relaxed a notch—Gerry seemed calmer now and he was more or less mirroring my own thoughts. I knew that leaving would mean either a straight surrender to police or fighting through the mob outside, and at that moment I didn't fancy our chances with either. We really didn't have much of a choice.

"Okay. For the record, I'm not convinced by this place—but we'll stay here for now and see what happens." I scanned the dancefloor again. "At least the folk seem friendly enough."

Then Gerry raised his finger as if something had just occurred to him. "Hang on," he said, "can you see anyone with a mobile phone in here?"

He had a point, "Now you mention it—no, I don't."

"Ahh, *bonjour,* gentlemen!" a voice purred at us from behind the bar. We both turned and saw a barman had materialised just as suddenly as the two girls had earlier. He was a heavy-set, middle aged man with cropped hair dressed in a black Tuxedo. He smiled widely and peered at us through thick-rimmed glasses, his hands clasped expectantly in front of him. He was awaiting our orders.

"Uh, can I have two—err—medium bodied chardonnays please," I said. "And two beers."

"Beers?" the Barman looked quizzical.

"Yes, some bottled lager please? You know, Millers, Stella, Bud—something like that?"

"Ah, yes. It's just that—well, we don't have a terribly large amount of beer in stock, sir. Tell me, are you invited guests?" The barman's accent was an uncomfortable mix of BBC English and a hint of west coast brogue—it sounded put on. I struggled to think of the best way to explain our presence in the Club. "Err, yes. Keisha and, err..."

"Teagan," said Gerry.

"They met us outside when we were walking by and—well, they asked us to come in."

"Ah right, I see," said the Barman. "Well, if you'll excuse me one moment, I'll just have a wee look down the stairs and see what we've got." The Barman then lurched off around the corner of the bar and ducked down through a low, narrow door which I presumed led to a cellar.

"A bar with no beer," said Gerry, "this place is a threat right enough."

I used the break to look around again, I didn't like the way there only seemed to be one way in or out of the place. As I did this, the bass thump died down and the music took a bizarre left turn as 'Would?', an old Alice in Chains track began to play. Jeez, I loved that song. It seemed an odd choice for the company there, but I wasn't complaining.

More bodies both young and old moved onto the dance floor and began to sway to the hypnotic riff.

"Sorry, gents I do apologise," the well-spoken Barman said as he returned behind us, "we're all out of beer and such this evening. I'm afraid we only have a few spirits and porters left, as well as our special selections of wine, of course. We do only tend to provide drinks which directly complement the food."

Gerry turned to me in dismay, mouthing the words 'Help me...'

"Fine, we'll have two of the same then," I said. "Let's not complicate things."

"Ah, an excellent choice, sir," the barman glowed. "The acidity in the Chardonnay does complement the food most exquisitely. Let's see, the house Chardonnay at the moment is a particularly pleasant, err..." he turned around and lifted a bottle from a collection at the back of the bar, glancing at the label as he did so, "...this one," he beamed.

The guy clearly had no idea, he was winging it. With that, he began to empty the contents of the bottle into four glasses. He flamboyantly threw the empty bottle spinning into a large, plastic rubbish bin near the cellar door and placed the glasses in front of us. Gerry handed him the twenty.

"Oh, no no no," said the Barman, sweeping the money away. "Did my young friends not explain the monetary arrangements?"

"No," I said, "is it all on a tab or something?"

Or could I be right about the bait club scam?

"Oh no sir, this is an entirely private party tonight. All refreshments are provided and are complimentary for the guests—it's one of our traditions. The Club is largely a co-operative you see, run by subscription so we don't have to worry about bar and food prices on the night."

"So, there's food too?" asked Gerry.

"Yes, of course," the barman continued, with a grin so seamless and sincere it only made me more nervous.

"If you've just joined us then I'm afraid you've missed the cold starters, but I'm sure you'll be fully included throughout the rest of the evening."

Gerry looked to me and smiled, "See? It's fine. Like the girls said, it's a private function, these folks have just hired the place out for a party. I think we've actually landed on our feet here, mate."

That explanation fitted of course, and it did seem to make sense. Maybe I was just being paranoid.

Then something caught my eye. As I glanced over at the main entry to the Club, there was a sudden movement through the windows in the double doorway—but then it was gone. I stilled myself and watched. And there it was again, a dark, frantic movement—and then it passed. Something dark flashed past the windows in the reception under the ultraviolet glow of the Club sign.

Another movement, a sudden glimpse of what could have been an angry face at one of the windows. I was too far away to see any detail. Could that have been one of the doormen from earlier? I nudged Gerry and nodded towards the doors so we had two pairs of eyes on whatever was happening.

However, as soon as Gerry caught on, more and more bodies suddenly seemed to want to get up and dance mid song, restricting our view to nothing more than an occasional glance. From our obscured view, all I could then see were impressions of moving silhouettes. Then, after a few seconds, the window cleared, all movement stopped—and no one came through the doors.

I spoke quietly, "Did you see any of that? Looked like some sort of scuffle outside. If we're staying here we should make ourselves discreet." Gerry nodded quietly, understood. He picked up two wine glasses and followed on as I skirted around the outside of the dance floor, making my way to a seating alcove I had spotted opposite the entrance. From there we had a clear view of the only confirmed way in—but it was also far enough away to give us a heads up if any trouble came through them.

We sat down at a wooden table surrounded by five wooden chairs which probably would have looked less out of place in a grandparent's hallway than a back-street nightclub. My chair creaked and complained as I rested my weight on its frame. We placed our drinks down and sat in silence for a minute or so just listening to the music and watching the doors to see if any trouble came through them.

Eventually Gerry spoke. "Okay, this whole shitstorm—I've been thinking about it." I moved forward to hear what he was saying, my chair groaned accordingly.

"Sorry, sometimes I forget how things get done in the real world. I've been trying to put that fight out of my head all night but it's hopeless, those guys were twats, but they weren't the enemy. That shouldn't have happened. You're right, soon as we leave here we should go to the police."

I nodded quietly, "You know it is."

"I mean, it was an accident, and it was one of them who pulled the blade—and that was way out of order in anyone's books, even if I was giving them a hard time. I mean, those guys are doormen—but they're supposed to have some sort of code, right?"

I nodded again, I was still having a hard time believing what had happened myself.

"I know I went off at them, but that was self-defence, right?"

"The whole incident was an outrage, and you didn't help. But yes, it was necessary force, to protect you and me both. It won't make things any easier though, we'll still get a rough ride, and that's only with the civvy police for starters."

"Yeah, but we don't want to make things look even worse by running away, do we? Well, any more than we have done already. Look, I'll happily take the hit for arguing with them as long as you tell the cops you saw them pull the knife."

"Gerry, all we need to tell them is the truth. Those guys on the doors are supposed to be professionals, pulling a blade on some bellend just for insulting them is way off the scale."

Gerry nodded, he rolled with the insult graciously but neither of us felt much like bantering. We were both hunched forward at the table now. I found I still couldn't take my eyes off the doors where I saw the commotion happening earlier.

"Okay. There's something else," said Gerry, "but I'd be breaking the principle by telling you, so if you don't want to hear, say now."

We both knew well what he meant by 'the principle', our mutual agreement not to mention anything in our previous military lives. We masked it by calling it 'the Basil principle' after the old episode of Fawlty Towers where 'don't mention the war' became a catch phrase.

Keeping your mouth closed about work had always been essential, but since 9/11 everything had changed, there were ears everywhere and it only needed one idiot and a social media account to drop us deeply in the shit, so to us it was no sitcom joke.

I looked around, no one seemed to be in hearing range and the music was most likely too loud for anyone else to listen in, as long as we were quiet. It was a risk though, it was always a risk. I made the call.

"I'm guessing you've got a good reason. Make it quick and keep it quiet, And, I know a lot of it still gets to you—so if you start losing it on me we shut it down, understood?"

Gerry nodded, we both knew the principle was for our own good. He leaned in a little closer and spoke a little more quietly.

"That last tour we were on, you know, none of the false flag stuff we got dragged into before?"

I nodded again, at least he didn't want to talk about stuff that could get us murdered just for mentioning it.

"That evac we did outside Deshu." I felt my own back tingling—all of those memories were hurt, but especially that last one. It was still with me too, but I nodded him on; he needed to get something out.

"I know we've talked it to death and—it's not as big a button for me as it once was," his brow furrowed; he looked as if he was choosing his words carefully.

"You know, we got those girls out of the compound, we got them through the desert in the dark—we were almost at the RV—then we saw..." he paused, "you know, the extra girl?"

I nodded, just the mention of it took me back there too. I knew what was coming, but I needed to know what his point was.

"Then things went critical, we didn't even have time to think. I went into autopilot, and can't even remember doing what I did—but I do remember the sound of the girls screaming when they realised they were going to die."

By that time, I was watching him carefully. It had been a horrific experience, one of those moments of horror which would never leave either of us.

"Do you remember I couldn't get that sound out of my head—like—at all?"

I nodded nervously and quickly scanned around for anyone who might be looking our way. Thankfully there was no one I could see.

"Yeah, I know, the sound of it was worse than any of the shrapnel. It's still with me too."

"It was. But as you know, with the docs and the meds and a lot of time—the screams had all died down. Just before the summer there I had pretty well buried it all, they weren't even waking me up anymore."

I still wasn't sure where he was going with it all

"Right, I said."

"Well, I'm more than happy to be in this place tonight, and I know I argued the case for staying earlier. But ever since we came in, just after we stepped in those front doors, I swear I've started to hear those screams again. It's like they're still in the back of my head somewhere, but they've been slowly pushing their way back out front again..."

I raised my hand, he had said enough, not just about the war, but about the Club too. I remembered the moment we had in the reception area, almost like a shared bad vibe. Gerry was right, the doorman aside, none of the crowd in there seemed much of a threat, but I knew that if the place or the situation was affecting him like that, we were going to have to get out of there soon.

"Okay," I said, "I get it and I'm with you, we can't stay here long."

He nodded, we both understood.

"Don't worry," he said, "I'm doing what we always do, pushing them all back down where they should be. But they're still there..."

We sat in silence a few seconds more, then he took a deep breath, as if returning back to his usual self.

"So, how long do we wait till we make our excuses?" he asked.

I studied him a few seconds longer, but he seemed to have come around. I ran the options in my head, what was our best strategy? I looked at my watch, it said 02:10hrs.

"This place won't be open forever, I reckon we wait till three when it'll probably close, and then all the streets will get busy. By that time, the bonehead will be in the hospital."

"Or the morgue," Gerry added. My mind fell back to the hissing sound of the breath escaping from the doorman's chest. He had a valid point, but I wasn't going to reinforce it, things were bad enough.

"Also, the police should have the whole place, including the lynch mob under control, and they'll be guaranteed to be looking for us. They're bound to have spoken to Norman, the twat who pulled the knife in the first place."

"As if he's going to tell them what really happened..."

"Right, so the police will want us bad—so we'll go straight to them. I reckon when we leave here we walk straight back down to Lady's along the main roads—no closes or dark passageways. The place will be crawling with cops now. We will get a hard time—especially if Norman got his story in first—but at least if we're with them we should be safe."

"Okay. But what if the cops come in here looking for us?"

I sat back in my chair, "We tell them the truth; we were chased in here and were too scared to come out."

"What about that guy you saw in reception a few minutes ago?"

I turned around again to see if anything was happening behind the doors—there was no sign of movement. Had I been mistaken? After all, the light was low and my mind was in overdrive. I shrugged. "If the mob storms in we'll just have to play it by ear—get out as quick as we can."

"You mean run like girls?"

Oh, for fuck's sake Gerry, get a grip, I thought to myself. But we were both hardwired not to run or step down from conflict, it was a hard habit to break and was a stigma in the forces.

"Yeah, that's exactly what we'll do, because we're civilians. Unless you want in deeper?"

Gerry nodded. I wasn't going to point out that, trauma issues or not, it was his arsehole attitude that had landed us here in the first place. Anyway, as we spoke I realised we had probably both sobered up a few notches since the fight at Lady's, and that was a bonus. I knew we would have to stay that way to cope with whatever happened next.

"We better make these our last," I said. Gerry agreed.

As we sipped our drinks cautiously I still couldn't stop glancing over at those double doors.

Then the music crunched and changed again.

This time it was Garbage, I think I'm *Paranoid*.

Very funny, I thought.

8. Secrets

And the music played on. The dancefloor became even busier as more and more bodies filtered out from other unseen parts of the Club.

"The girls have been gone a long time," said Gerry. He was right, they had been gone an age.

"Where did they say they were off to?" he asked.

"Wasn't it the bathroom?"

Could it be they had brought us in here then just bailed?

But then, as if on perfect cue, the reception doors swung open and both girls walked in. I watched as they skirted around the dance floor, stopping briefly by the DJ booth where Teagan spoke again to the guy running the decks. A few seconds later both were back at our table where they pulled up chairs and sat down.

"Are these ours?" asked Keisha, glancing at the two full glasses of wine. "Thank you, sirs."

The girls picked up their glasses in unison and sipped at the pale liquid.

"Is everything alright out there?" I asked.

"Sorry?" said Teagan, as she made eye contact, slowly running her tongue along her lower lip. I tried not to notice it.

"Out by the front door. I saw some sort of commotion through the glass earlier on—didn't realise you guys were out there, we thought you were both in the bathroom?"

"Oh, we were," said Keisha, "But you can walk all the way round to the front door from the bathrooms without having to come back into the main hall. It's like a circular route outside, all these foundation arches, it's a real warren in here."

"Yeah, in all it's a very cool venue," Teagan added with an enthusiastic grin.

"So, there was no trouble?" I asked. I wasn't convinced.

"Oh no," said Keisha. "Well, Vincent did mention some guy tried to barge in earlier—but we're very strict on who we mingle with—he was turned around very quickly. It is a private party after all."

"I know, the barman told us," said Gerry.

"Really? What else did he tell you?" Teagan said, her voice natural but sudden, as if betraying an edge of urgency.

"Well..." started Gerry.

"Not much at all," I said. Maybe I was overreacting, but I didn't want to start repeating what others had said in the club—could be a recipe for disaster if there were personal politics and we said the wrong thing. If Teagan or Keisha didn't want us to know our full story, that was more than fine by me. I was happy to return the favour by not being nosy.

"There's really no great secret here," said Teagan. "We're all just acquaintances who get together every now and again for a bit of a gathering," she smiled.

"And—we come from all over," continued Keisha. "In fact, depending where the gathering is, there can be someone from just about every corner of the world. This is just a small get together tonight—most of us here have only travelled from Europe."

'Okay,' I said. I remembered the map in reception with pins in it—some kind of guest map maybe?

"So, we never really have a meeting in the same city or place twice in a row. It wouldn't be fair on everyone for the sake of travelling."

"Honestly, it feels like years since we were in Scotland—and we do love this part of town," smiled Teagan.

"So, what *do* you all have in common then?" Gerry asked. Again, maybe I was overreacting, but I had been hoping that he'd worked out that same theory of discretion I had.

"Well, we're all friends for one thing..." offered Keisha. Weak answer.

"Yes, I gathered, but *why* are you all friends?" asked Gerry. "What puts you all together?"

Not an unreasonable question in the circumstances. Keisha and Teagan looked at each other as if exchanging thoughts. They kept smiling but it began to look practised. Awkward moment it seemed.

"Well?"

"Gerry, please shut up," I said with a smile. "You're beginning to piss everyone off."

He shrugged. There was a short silence at the table punctuated only by the onset of tribal drumming and distinctive guitar riffs—Killing Joke now—really? Good call, but another strange choice I thought—or maybe they just liked their alt rock. At that moment I realised almost every track they'd played since we came in had been a favourite of mine at one time or another. That was weird in itself, especially for this part of town where the music was often generic, singalong, crowd-pleasing fluff.

Teagan gave me a quick look of thanks and then turned to Gerry, "It's really not a big deal," she said. "If anything, the main reason is actually a bit dull, maybe even embarrassing. It's a genealogy thing."

Our blank looks prompted her further, "Family trees. Most of the people here can all trace their genealogy back to a certain time and place—so I suppose you could say we're all family in some way. You know, we're not all related but we are loosely connected through history, so we have some things in common. We're kind of nostalgic, so that connection is something we like to hold on to in this day and age."

Keisha nodded, "And we're a very difficult group to fall in with. In fact, you two should be honoured to be in here, very few outsiders are ever invited into Medusa."

"Yes! But *why*?" said Gerry, smiling, I knew his head was probably fried by what had happened earlier but if this was him attempting cheeky humour then it was the wrong time and place.

"We're also very private in some ways," Keisha said, suddenly icy. "This is our social event, our nightclub. If you want to stay and join in—then we'll explain as we go." Then she smiled, "I'm sure you wouldn't want to leave early, would you?" She directed this at Gerry, "Those gents we saw outside did seem very keen to speak to you?" Her tone wasn't threatening but her words were barely veiled.

I leaned over to Gerry and whispered, "What she means, shithead, is don't ask—and then neither will they. Now shut the fuck up and just enjoy being safe for a little bit longer, okay?"

Gerry got the point. "Okay, sorry ladies, trying to be funny here. Please ignore me, I'm an arse." His defusing left a lot to be desired but it would do. He sat back, retreating behind his glass. But to me, Keisha's sudden tone had confirmed it—there was definitely something else going on in there. All we could do was hope that whatever it was, we wouldn't be dragged into it—whatever it might be.

I jumped into the conversation to try and change the subject, "The barman said you do food at your parties too—sounded like a big deal to you all?"

"Oh, yes—that's the whole point of the night really," said Keisha, all traces of iciness now gone, "a good wholesome, evening's entertainment really, just like the music—something for everyone."

"And as we said, if you would like to stay, you really are most welcome to join us for what's left of the night," said Teagan.

"Sure—of course," I said, putting on my bravest face.

"Do you often eat so late though?" Gerry asked.

"Yes—it might seem strange for us Brits but most other cultures eat much later on in the evening anyway, and many of the guests aren't acclimatised to being a few hours behind yet. It just seems easier to go with what they're used to, so we let them set the pace."

"Again, it's just being fair to everyone," said Keisha.

Complete bullshit answer, I thought, *if these people were Europeans, no one would be more than two hours ahead, and it's already after two in the morning.*

"It *is* a bit of a fucking drag though, I'm famished..." deadpanned Teagan. She caught Keisha's eye and both burst into a fit of girlish giggles which belied their vampish looks. Gerry looked at me as if asking for approval to converse again after his verbal time out. I shrugged and rolled my eyes. We were absolutely in a world of shit on the outside and I was pretty sure we were being lied to—but maybe I really was being overly paranoid. We did need to leave, but a few more minutes surely wouldn't hurt. Deal with all the bad stuff later, right?

And so, with the ice broken and only a few minor stalls, we all began easily chatting. So easily in fact that it was bizarre. As the conversation turned to our backgrounds we found out about the monotony of Keisha's job as an actuary in London and Teagan's medical studies in Dublin, which she financed by working the evenings as an 'off the books' private hire driver. Suddenly they both seemed very normal and very easy company.

When it came to our turn, both Gerry and I gave them our rehearsed and vague and slightly embellished back stories about having been squaddies once upon a time, then happily returning to civvy life after little incident and with no issues. Thankfully neither girl pushed or questioned any of it.

As we talked though, I noticed the girls seemed to want to up the pace of the drinking. Was that a bad thing? Yes, it was. Even with the best intentions, all my best laid plans of staying sharp and leaving at a specific time were soon falling by the wayside. I surmised they must have had some kind of eye contact going with the barman, who seemed to appear strategically every time the levels in our glasses dropped.

Along with everything else this just added to the level of surreal. We had both been through a horrific trauma that night—someone might be dead—yet there we were, drinking and chatting with a couple of new friends just as if none of it had happened. I knew it was wrong, or sick, or something, but I wasn't complaining, there was no point. Maybe it was only because I knew we were delaying the inevitable circus of interviews when we left.

As we drank, talked and laughed the time rolled on and the music seemed to become more linear, the changes smoother. Maybe the DJ was getting the hang of his gear. We heard an odd and varied selection of sounds, from the previous favourites from Garbage and Killing Joke to Morissette, Sinatra and Nirvana by way of Bobby Goldsboro and P.J. Harvey—Bauhaus via Linkin Park, Britney and Siouxsie—diverse was too mild a word for it.

In some ways the playlist seemed to add to the ease of being there for me, it was all so familiar. I guessed the DJ was probably on some kind of psychedelics, but in those strange surroundings and to my drunk and whacked out ears it all made musical sense. And I still knew every song. Weird? Yes, it was—but I listen to all kinds of music, so probably just all happy coincidence. Maybe all these folks were just on my wavelength?

When I pushed her on it, Teagan explained that everyone brought some music of their own (CDs or vinyl only) so the eclectic playlist was mostly down to a nominated DJ trying to make it work on hired equipment with a whole bunch of music they may not be familiar with. Sounded plausible, if slightly on the lame side.

But as the time passed and the wine began to dull everything further, I realised my own guard was beginning to drop—and strangely, I found I didn't care. What was done was done—what lay ahead was still in the future, right? Somehow, the reluctance I'd had about this club, the bad vibes, the nagging feeling that something wasn't right—they were all gradually wearing away. I also couldn't help but notice that Gerry seemed to be getting on very well with Teagan—not just in a 'successfully chatted her up' way, but as if they were connecting really well—as if they were actually on each other's wavelengths. Weird though that may be, knowing Gerry. Who knew? If nothing else good came from this tonight, then maybe he'd finally found someone who was a foil for his demons? It was a thought.

Eventually I asked Keisha about the name, "So why Medusa? Is there a story there?"

"Ha, yes," she laughed, "though it's all a bit obscure. Well, firstly, some of the olds here claim to be able to trace their roots as far back as Marco Polo's days, to a tribe of Sumatrans, believe it or not, who were apparently quite notorious at the time, so I gather,"

"In what way?"

"Umm, I couldn't really say... You know what olds are like with their secrets, not exactly very forthcoming around us youngsters—so we just enjoy the social side and leave the dusty stuff to them."

"Okay, I get that—but why Medusa?"

"Oh, I know this!" said Teagan. "There's an old painting in The Louvre..."

"Yes, 'The Raft of the Medusa,' said Keisha. "There was disaster at sea about two hundred years ago, a ship called the Medusa sank and, from what they tell us, most of the olds in the Club can trace their ancestry back to surviving on the raft after the shipwreck."

"So," said Teagan, "this disaster was awful and a real scandal in its day. The Captain was blamed for the sinking and most of the crew died. The ones who survived lived through all sorts of horrors and to make things worse, they were very harshly judged afterwards. So, this Club was started in secret as the people of the day were, err—less than understanding. But the whole thing has just kept going—and even though it's a closely guarded secret, we still seem to keep gaining new members. We both think that's probably because of the way the world is today."

"The way *people* are today," said Keisha

What the fuck? That wasn't a clear answer in anyone's books, it probably raised even more questions if anything. But her eyes told me she was finished on the subject, so it seemed best to leave it at that.

"All sounds a bit like the bloody masons to me," said Gerry.

"Honestly," said Keisha, "there's nothing unnatural going on here, we're all quite open—to certain people. The exclusive side is more to do with everyone's privacy and carrying on certain traditions and heritage."

"And all of that is way too dull and philosophical for banter at a disco, believe me. But you're not too far off the mark, what's that tagline the Masons have these days? Not a secret society, but a society with secrets?"

She sounded vaguely patronising, as if she were trying to make out the whole idea was above our heads. Okay, fine. And for the record, 'unnatural' was a strange choice of word.

"I see..." I said, maybe a little too slowly. "Maybe a chat for another time then."

Keisha smiled, "Okay, later then," as her eyes lingered on mine longer than they maybe should have. I shifted uncomfortably in my seat; I wasn't quite sure where all of it was leading.

9. Gone

Before long the aroma of freshly cooked food was in the air. The smell made me realise how long it was since I had last eaten and my stomach began to anticipate the thought of doing so again. My eye was drawn to someone approaching the table, a distinguished middle-aged man in a dark suit and tie. He stood behind the remaining empty chair which creaked as he rested his hands on its back. As they closed around the wood I noticed his fingernails were all manicured into fine points.

"May I?" he asked, his eyes trawling slowly around us.

"Of course, Pierre," said Keisha. The man sat down and clasped his hands on the table in front of him with the seasoned air of a TV news presenter. He smiled looking all around the table as Keisha introduced him, "Gerry, Paul, this is Pierre, he's our trusty organiser. He's also the executive head chef and wine buyer—it's him you really have to thank for all this hospitality tonight." Pierre nodded an acknowledgement to us both. We both graciously nodded back.

"Good evening, my friends," Pierre said in a deep, overdramatic tone, like some scenery chewing stage actor. Like the Barman earlier, it sounded put on to me.

"The girls here have already told me about you—good of you to join us so late in the evening."

Jesus, this gets weirder every minute, I thought.

"Oh, really, it's our pleasure," I said, aware I was playing along. This was really becoming a bit too much—if all these people were playing some kind of charade, then Pierre's pretence and pointy manicure were almost enough to edge me over into the plain pissed off territory. I wasn't sure how much more of this patronising drama I could take, private party or not. I also couldn't help but notice Pierre's dark eyes lingering over both Gerry and me for longer than I thought was polite.

"Please forgive my intrusion, I just wanted to let you know *personally* that the next course will be served within the next few minutes."

Keisha and Teagan both grinned widely, "Superb!" Keisha beamed. The girls were like putty in his hands—he was obviously one of the top dogs here.

His brief act over, Pierre stood up and smoothly walked off into the lights and clamour of the dancefloor, leaving Gerry and me watching his departure with vaguely puzzled looks.

"Pierre doesn't sound very French to me," Gerry said, eventually.

"Oh, but he is," said Teagan, "I know him well. He was born in France, but came to this country when he was young. He went to a very exclusive school in the Highlands somewhere, so... err..." she faltered, "...I suppose he won't have much of an accent left. But he really is wonderful at organising these nights for us. He has all the best connections and ideas and he's always willing to throw in a few surprises."

At that, the music faded and the muffled voice of the DJ was heard for the first time through the speaker system, "Ladies and Gentlemen, umm—it's my pleasure to announce that the next course is now being served."

Then the lights came up—but that wasn't saying much. The extra brightness only went far enough to lighten the middle of the room, leaving most of the outlying snugs and alcoves still shrouded in shadow. The girls stood up and began making their way to the buffet table at the far side of the room, and we quickly followed them. Complete strangers smiled and nodded at us on our way as we joined the short queue leading to the table.

The table itself was lit by a square, overhanging box light which looked as if it may have served over a snooker or pool table in a previous life—but the spread it illuminated was exquisite. From where I stood I could see that when it came to feeding themselves, these people, whoever they were, spared no expense. There were no sausage rolls or hurriedly defrosted vol-au-vents here.

My stomach felt empty as my eyes took in the beautifully presented selections of thinly cut cold and cooked meats, both smooth and coarse, red and white with selections of salads, fruit and bread and an assortment of bowls filled with thick, dark dips and sauces. Not being much of a foodie myself I could only have guessed at what half this stuff might have been—but it looked and smelled delicious. Between the exertion of our earlier experience and the steady flow of wine through the evening, I found I was now almost ravenous with hunger.

Then Gerry tapped me on the shoulder, "Hey—see those two guys helping themselves to that venison type stuff up ahead?" he said, pointing to two well-dressed thirtysomethings in the midst of filling their plates.

"I see them."

"I recognise them. I'm pretty sure they're doctors, or something medical at least. I've seen them in the hospital before."

"Really? Are you sure?"

"Yeah—well, fairly. They look familiar—I wouldn't know their names, you know what it's like with my job, different faces all day long..."

"Do you think they might be able to shed any light on this lot?"

"Dunno. I'll rack my brain and see if I can't remember where they're from. I'll see if I can think of some way to start some sort of chat with them without getting their backs up."

You'd be lucky, I thought.

The queue moved quickly and I watched the girls, following their lead. They moved eagerly and expertly as if they knew the food, garnishing each with particular vegetables and sauces. I took similar choices and combinations onto my own plate—I didn't want to look too much like a novice.

Our food selected, we returned to the table to find yet another bottle of Chardonnay opened for us there. Shit.

As we sat and began to eat, I caught sight of Pierre standing by a distant doorway watching keenly over the proceedings with a grin. He caught sight of me watching him back and smiled, his expression never faltering.

"This is pretty good," I heard Gerry say, through a mouthful of half chewed meat.

"Sorry?" I realised I had been distracted.

"The food..." said Gerry, "...it's good."

"Oh, right," I whispered. "Best enjoy it, we're going to have a long weekend once we get out of here,"

"Oh, give me a break," he moaned. He was right though; the food was delicious.

Both girls ate silently, as if in reverence, clearing almost everything from their plates before passing any comment.

"Excellent, good old Pierre, up to his usual standards!" said Keisha. Teagan smiled and nodded in delighted agreement between sips of wine.

After a while, our empty plates were collected by a group of jovial older women and men who scurried around the tables looking vaguely surreal in ill-fitting waiters' and maids' outfits. Strangely, they all wore white, half face eye masks, similar to the full face with red smears below the eyes I saw hanging outside the Club. They removed all the plates and cutlery from around the tables and alcoves with breathtaking speed and efficiency, then wiped down all the surfaces with cloths that smelled of lemon and disinfectant. It all appeared very thorough, very swift.

Then just as we began some more small talk with the girls, the DJ cranked the music back on with raucous meanderings I recognised straight away as being early Radiohead. What was that guy singing—an *airbag* saved his life? I always wondered, never checked. Why was I even thinking that? The alcohol was beginning to send my mind off in odd tangents...

Gerry dabbed his mouth with a napkin obviously trying to make a good impression, then placed it on top a pile of plates being collected by our own maid. She looked at us all in turn—she was smiling, but the mask over her upper face only made her look blank and disturbing. Then with a stack of dishes in hand, she paused and began chatting to the girls about all the best sights to see while they were in town. The Castle, the Museum, the Cove at Gilmerton especially, Mary King's Close and a few others I didn't quite catch.

Gerry leaned over towards me and spoke quietly, "You know, I think I do know where I've seen those guys before," he said. But Teagan's ears pricked up at this and she broke away from her chat with the maid, "Oh—you've seen someone here you know?" she asked excitedly.

Gerry turned to her, "Well, I *think* I might have—remember I told you I worked in the hospital? Well, I thought I saw a couple of the clinical guys in here who work in the wards. I wasn't quite sure where at first, but I think it's finally come to me..." Both girls were now eagerly sitting forward and seemed to be hanging on to his every word. Gerry looked taken aback by their interest.

"Uh, I usually see them when I take the patients into theatre, I'm pretty sure they're anaesthetists."

"Really!" said Keisha, looking excitedly at Teagan. Teagan turned back round to Gerry.

"Well, we do know most of the people who come to these nights, but we don't always know about their day work. Why don't we go over and speak to them?" she said, "Imagine not knowing something like that." She turned to Keisha, "Would you look after Paul while we're gone, sweetie?" Something unspoken seemed to pass between the two girls as they smiled at each other. Keisha looked over at me and moistened her lips with the tip of her tongue. It seemed that, even through the haze of the strong wine, somehow the evening's events had taken yet another strange turn.

"Of course, I'd *love* to..." said Keisha, too slowly, too deliberately.

"Come on Gerry, let's have a wander around," said Teagan as she stood up and began moving towards the dance floor. Gerry stood up, helping her move her own chair out the way in a mock gentlemanly manner. Despite everything I could tell just by the way he moved around her that he seemed enraptured - in his mind he had probably scored big time, but I did hope there might be something more there.

"So, did you see where your friends went?" I heard Teagan ask as she led him off into the strobe lights.

"No, I can't see them now, they must be sitting in the dark somewhere..." their voices merged into the music and then became lost. I saw Teagan turn to him—then she took his hand and both disappeared off into the darkness of the alcoves and recesses.

10. Promise

"Maybe you'd like a little more wine?" Keisha purred. She was looking at me differently now, there had been a definite switch. Her eyes seductively narrow, her lips parted and glistening. Before I could answer she was already pouring more strong, pale drink into my glass. I nodded dumbly, I wasn't in much of a mind to argue anymore; the slow intoxication of strong wine, good food and attractive female company had already skewed my sensibility, even though it went against every lesson I had ever learned.

Although my mind was by then mostly focused on staying out of harm's way, that pointless, stupid fight. It had drawn a strong line of unease through everything that had happened since. I was still worried about Gerry too. Whether he was to blame or not, he took the full brunt of the trauma and been fully freaked earlier. He still wasn't out of the woods yet, and now I had lost sight of him in this dark, disorienting basement.

I also hadn't been able to shake the feeling of dread at our imminent involvement with the law, both civilian and military which I knew would be blindsiding us soon. But despite everything, I found I was pushing all that out of my head just to be there with Keisha in that moment.

It was plain from the outset these girls were charismatic and attractive, but it wasn't until I found myself close enough to inhale her perfume that I realised I had become fascinated by Keisha's enticing air of suggestive sex. As I thought clearly for the first time about the possibility of getting intimate with her, I realised I was probably far enough gone to do anything she might ask just to be able to take things that far. I mean, after tonight my whole future was most likely screwed anyway, why not screw it up some more?

She slid her chair along the floor, closer to my side. As she did so I realised I could sense her above all the other sweet sensations in the room. My stomach fluttered as she reached over and stroked the inside of my leg through my jeans.

"You know what? I think we could end up being *really* close friends, you and I," she whispered. I looked into her eyes and they seemed aglow. I felt a stirring between my legs.

(No—damn, there was something else—the last thing I needed—one thing was going to stop all this.)

"Well... did you enjoy the meal?" she whispered slowly, in close to me—I felt my head rush, stirred by her warm breath at my ear.

(Christ no—I knew I was going to blow it—I couldn't help myself.)

"Yes..." I was already beginning to feel stupid, angry at myself for having to ruin the moment before I even mentioned it.

"I'm *so* glad we met, you know..."

(No, I couldn't put it off any longer.)

"So am I—" I was cut short as I felt the warm softness of her tongue as she leaned in close and lightly teased it along my earlobe, my whole body tingled as I felt the moist trail on my skin cool under her breath...

(Oh God, here goes.)

"Keisha—I'm *really* sorry but I'm going to have to leave you for a few seconds."

"Ohhh—really?" she complained breathily in my ear. I sighed, hating myself for it—it was so typically me.

"I feel so stupid but—can you tell me where the gents' bathroom is?"

To my relief, she leaned back slightly and chuckled. Under the table her hand moved slowly over my leg to squeeze my hand in turn.

"Of course," she smiled, "I totally understand—if you've gotta go..."

I gave her an apologetic smile. With the conflicting sensations of discomfort and longing in my groin, I could clearly feel my want for this girl overtaking every other thought I had—and that sort of thing never happened to me. Nevertheless, she seemed oblivious to my poor timing and her eyes remained fixed on mine even though she knew I had just blown the flow.

"You would be quickest going through those double doors and then turn to the left, you'll see it just a little way along that corridor," she said. "There's a sign."

"Thanks."

"You won't be long, will you?"

"No way, I promise."

"Good," she smiled. "And don't get lost."

"Don't worry—just hold that thought."

"I will. And I mean it about getting lost, some of this place... Well, it's a bit dark and dangerous in parts and I'm afraid Pierre doesn't care much for Health and Safety."

I nodded, smiled and tore myself away from her gaze, breaking off the touch of our hands as I stood up and walked towards the doors. Until that moment I hadn't even realised we had been holding hands, it was almost as if I'd completely forgotten myself, my situation, my life...

Walking across the empty dancefloor (I guess Radiohead had never really been floor fillers), I was again thrown occasional waves and smiles from strangers who happened to catch my eye. I did my best to return the acknowledgements even though it felt wrong.

There was so much going on in my head right then—between the alcohol, the food, the atmosphere in the Club and that surge of lust for Keisha which had surprised and overtaken me, everything seemed to have meshed to create some sort of sudden, intoxicating euphoria for life and the moment. By then I had almost lost sight of why I was in their Club in the first place, it was almost as if I had some kind of blinkered focus telling me that nothing else mattered. I wondered if it was some kind of trauma survival instinct kicking in.

I opened the double doors and glanced back, only to see that in my absence Pierre had scuttled straight over to Keisha and was now stooped down, talking in her ear. Keisha nodded sporadically as if agreeing with different points. I shrugged it off, turned around and saw Vincent, the doorman from earlier, standing sentry in a corner of the reception area brooding in the ultraviolet. I nodded to him—he acknowledged me with the least possible effort and continued to stand impassively as if in a time and space all of his own, waiting for the next distraction from this world to intrude.

Following Keisha's directions, I turned left, walking a few yards down a musty corridor with a string of lightbulbs running along it. I saw that after the first few, they had all failed. Behind me I heard the sound of Radiohead fading and the upbeat intro as another track began. I couldn't hear exactly what it was as the doors were now closed and all I could hear was lower frequency of the beat.

After a few more paces along the dark and curved passageway I saw a distempered wooden door with an A4 piece of paper tacked to the outside panel. It read, 'Gentlemen's Bathroom,' in the fanciful flourish of a calligrapher. Someone clearly cared about the occasion of taking a piss.

Pushing the door open, I found the room aglow with flickering light from countless candles, tealights and incense sticks standing in glasses, melted on to bottle tops and carefully arranged around the flat surfaces in the room. It was impressive—a soft and relaxing chillout after the strobes and glare of the Club. But in the gentle glow I could still see a line of badly stained urinals and a couple of toilet cubicles with the doors broken on their hinges.

Even through the pleasant musk of the incense, there was a sharp tang of sewage in the air. Seemed like someone had done their best to overwrite the smell. The candlelight reflected warmly against the far wall where a row of mirrors hung over the wash-hand basins. This might have been a decent bathroom at one time, but now it was seriously neglected however hard you tried to mask it. Still, the place had a calming and strangely comforting effect and I suppose Pierre wouldn't have had time to fix everything.

I made for the nearest urinal bowl and began to empty my bladder in relief. I stood and slowed my breath as the liquid filtered out, shaking off some of that drink fuelled compliance I had felt with Keisha earlier as the discomfort inside released. Jeez, what had I been thinking? I had never been in shit so deep since the last time I'd worn a uniform—everything was properly messing with my head. This whole place was the opposite of what we'd seen earlier in the Bank Bar—everyone was so forthcoming, so accepting—yet I was none the wiser as to what was really going on.

I remembered how uneasy I felt just before we stepped through those doors, even though the place had been a godsend at the time. But it all just seemed *too* good, *too* lucky—and that's just not me, not by a long shot. Also, our companions, enigmatic and beautiful though they were, still hadn't come close to offering any decent explanation for this 'private party'. I shook my head slowly and felt my mind swirling heavily inside. This was no dream, it was all happening sure as I was standing there pissing, but it didn't add up—and that was sticking in my mind like a shard.

So even if I was grateful for all the sanctuary and hospitality, I wondered if an accidental wrong turn or two in the name of exploration may just have to be in order before I re-joined Keisha, even if only to put my mind at rest.

11. Served

As soon as I was finished I buttoned up my jeans and washed my hands in a basin which looked grimy, even in the candlelight. I picked up a bar of soap from the basin top but couldn't summon any hot water, so I resigned myself to using the cold. I winced as the freezing water poured between my fingers—but it sent a refreshing shiver through my body. Without any further thought I doused my face with it, hoping the sudden cold might just help shake off some of the intoxication and weirdness I was feeling. The effect was limited—the sensation rippled through me. The sudden drop in temperature was bracing and it helped, but my mind still felt clouded. I pondered the situation as I watched my cold, dripping features in the mirror.

But then, for the briefest of moments, the dull, distant pulse of the disco was overwritten by a sudden, muffled shriek, which, if my sense of direction was still reliable, had come directly from behind the wall in front of me. It had been a swift, sharp cry, but distinct enough—I hadn't imagined it. I turned my ear to the wall, straining to hear if I could pick anything else out.

And there it was again. I heard it clearly for a second time—shorter, more of a gasp that time. As before, it was as if the noise was coming from the next room just beyond the mirrored wall. All night my gut had been telling me something odd was going on in that place—I decided that it was now time to take a look.

Shaking the water from my face, I stepped out of the bathroom and brusquely glanced up and down the corridor. The smell of cooked food was much stronger there than in the Club, so presumably that meant I was closer to the kitchen. The passage outside the bathroom door curved away in both directions from where I stood and I guessed it may have circled out widely all the way around the main section of the Club.

The main entrance door and reception were beyond my line of sight and I judged that if anyone were to leave this bathroom and walk the other way, they would probably not be missed by Vincent, who seemed oblivious to everything last time I saw him. I closed the door as quietly as I could and walked down the corridor to my right, to where I assumed any access to that next room might be.

A few yards on, I saw the outline of a door in the wall. Its surface was cold, smooth and metallic like stainless steel, it looked like a kitchen door—this was it. I pressed my ear up against the metal and listened carefully. There were muffled voices beyond. The difference in pitch told me there was at least one male and one female talking on the other side—but the door seemed too thick and heavy to afford any clarity. The talking was punctuated by short outbursts of laughter and grunts of exertion, as if some couple were either having great fun lifting something heavy, or of course, getting frisky with each other. I quietly twisted the door handle—it wouldn't budge. Locked. Shit.

Just then I heard a sudden outpour of voices behind me in the reception area. I released the handle and backed off further down into the darkness of the corridor to get out of view, praying no one was going to walk my way. I held my breath as a brief and loud conversation passed between two girls about where the hell that arsehole barman had disappeared to just when he was needed most.

I exhaled slowly as I heard the voices carry off in the other direction. I presumed from the symmetry in the corridor that if the gents' bathroom was in this section, then the ladies' would most likely be down the other, and that was most likely where they had gone.

I stepped back to the outer wall and flanked further round into the dark, wondering if the kitchen might have another way in. After all, this had all probably been part of the same cellar at one time, and Keisha had said herself the place was like a warren. Maybe they had interconnecting doors—rooms inside leading to other rooms? Anything was possible.

With every step the light seemed to become less pronounced and the outlines less distinct—but I moved slowly, and my eyes seemed to adjust surprisingly quickly. I soon found I could make out vague shapes in the gloom. Again, I stole a glance behind me—if anyone were to use the men's bathroom now, they would most likely spot me lurking in the dark and I would be busted. So far though, the corridor seemed clear.

After maybe twenty feet or so of feeling my way along brick and plaster walls, I spotted the raised wood of what seemed like a door surround. I edged my fingers around the corner and felt them pass over external metal hinges—this was clearly another door. I placed my ear against it for a few seconds and held my breath. There were no sounds beyond, only the distant thump of music from the Club behind me and the occasional impressions of voices and laughter in the next room down. Whatever was happening in there was clearly still going on.

In the dark I could just make out some detail about the door—there was no handle, just a 'push' plate. I applied some pressure and found the door gave easily, opening inwards and releasing a faint stream of light from inside the room. I quickly slipped through the doorway, supporting the door, letting it swing gently closed behind me. A spring murmured as it travelled further out than the surround suggested it would and I realised it must have been mounted on double hinges with no stops to hold it. It was a two-way swing door—probably a main egress from the kitchen.

Inside the smell of food was even stronger, a sharp mix of garlic, onions and cooking steaks. I stood awkwardly against the wall and looked around the room. It was a sparse affair, and like the bathroom earlier it was lit by several large burning candle stubs melted onto the tops of empty bottles.

The only furniture in the room was a small, wooden dining table and grey swivel chair set against the farthest wall. On the table lay an open box of candles and a few matchboxes, their contents littered beside a pile of papers clamped together with bulldog clips. A large buttoned pocket calculator and some pens lay strewn about the desk as if it was some kind of admin base.

I walked quietly over to the desk and leafed through some of the notes. They were what I would have expected—receipts for wine, local vegetable supply, the hire of disco equipment, lights and a temporary dancefloor. Basically, the whole party as far as I could see, no surprises there. I held the bundle of papers under the candlelight and looked for more detail. Most had been signed by the purchaser but there were a whole bunch of different names on the agreements—and all had similar indecipherable handwriting. Didn't Keisha say that Pierre had organised all this himself? There was no sign of any Pierre's name in any of the admin.

I looked closer, trying to make out some of the scrawled autographs in the dim lighting and began to see names suggesting themselves: Mr Dahmer, Mr Sutcliff, Mr Nilsson—I knew those names somehow—those guys were all killers of some sort, right? It seemed as if the organiser wasn't keen on giving out real names and was probably trying to pass off some kind of black humour in the process.

"Sick bastards," I muttered aloud.

I pulled a few candles out of the box and stuffed them in my jacket pocket along with a handful of matches. I thought they might come in useful.

Looking around the room the only other features I could see were two dark jackets hanging on a row of coat hooks on to the far wall and a door in the wall adjacent, which looked as if it may connect to the room behind the wall in the bathroom. Crossing to the coat-hooks my stomach did a turn as I saw both were black flying jackets with 'Lady's Niteclub' embroidered on the front. These were just like the jackets worn by the bouncers chasing our tails earlier. Were those bastards down here in the Club? Could they all be in this together? Could it be the girls were only holding us there till they gathered their friends to pulp us? Maybe.

I decided it was time to leave. The only objective now was to find Gerry and get out, regardless of what may have been waiting for us outside. We could muse about all the weirdness at a later date from a safe distance.

But just at that moment, I heard a playful female drawl from behind the connecting door, "...but you know I *so like* to do it this way!" It was unmistakably Teagan's. I reasoned that if Teagan was in there, then so was Gerry. I was just going to have to interrupt and make my apologies.

I strode over to the doorway—but as I reached out to grip the handle, the door swung suddenly outwards, forced open by the burly frame of the Barman we met earlier. I stepped back out of the door's opening arc and saw he was carefully wiping the area around the corners of his mouth with a severely bloodied handkerchief. Had he hurt himself? Had somebody thumped him?

He held the door partially open and stopped, clearly surprised to see me there. But then he recovered himself and grinned widely, "Oh, I wouldn't go in there, sir," he said, quickly folding the handkerchief.

As I held his gaze I saw his eyes were open just slightly wider than they should be, his pupils maybe just a bit too dilated, even in the low light. There was something far more sinister to this guy than just that congenially polite exterior.

He must have read my intention before I moved as he stepped out of the doorframe and straight towards me, letting the door fall closed in the process. In a heartbeat I decided that the time for politeness had now passed, I need to get into that room to get Gerry out of it. I swiftly dipped down to his left and barged into him, sending him off balance, throwing myself into the gap between his bulk and the frame in the process. He began to stumble, off balance and surprised—and I was then directly in front of the door.

In the sudden movement he lost grip of the handkerchief. It caught my attention and I found myself watch it fall to the floor where it landed with an unpleasant, wet sound. I turned back and grabbed the door handle, but before I could pull it open, I felt his arm tightly lock around my neck from behind, hauling me viciously backwards.

"I told you—I *wouldn't* go in there!" This time his voice was heavy with threat. I jabbed back hard with my elbow and felt the blow connect solidly near the middle of his ribcage. The pressure dropped around my throat as the Barman then stumbled again and released his grip, again off centred and gasping. In a glance I saw he stumbled into a fall. He landed clumsily and rolled, probably winded—but I knew there was no going back after that, we had to move quickly.

I pulled the door open and stepped into the next room which was a much bigger and brighter space. I squinted—the sudden glare of florescent light and white tiled walls was dazzling after the dark corridors and candlelit bathroom. The smell of sweet, raw meat and cooking vegetables in here was overpowering—this was definitely the kitchen.

The room was a good size and it was lined with heavy-looking steel worktops and benches. The surfaces around the room were littered with arrangements of food in various states of preparation, obviously laid out and waiting their turn to be served up in the next course. Piled up next to the farthest away door there was a stack of black and blue plastic bags overflowing with empty containers and waste. To my left was a grid of industrial gas stoves where I saw steam rising from large steel pots where vegetables simmered and bobbed over the edges.

In the centre of the room were two freestanding metal trolleys, each supporting the remains of a large butchered carcass. The nearest seemed to be an entire skeleton side of beef; some unfortunate piece of cattle expertly picked and carved almost clean by a team of butchers.

But as I took a careful step towards the carcass I realised the ribs were far too small for the type of beast they surely must have belonged to. I drew closer and saw the upper part of the meat was covered with a torn plastic bag weighed down at either side with piles of curved and cleanly picked bones, some still linked by sinuous strands. It wasn't until I was close enough to fully see the proportions of the carcass that I realised, this was no piece of dead cattle; these remains were human.

Something inside wanted me to be sure. I reached over and—at full arm's length—slowly lifted the weighted piece of plastic away, exposing the head of the carcass. In that moment, every horror in my past, everything I thought I had processed, shaken off and rationalised welled up in my head when I saw what lay beneath it. Only part of the face remained, most of what was visible under a layer of dark, congealing blood and matter was the exposed bone of the skull, its empty eye socket peering lifelessly up at the underside of the bag.

What remained of the flesh had been neatly carved away from a point just below the chin to reveal features vaguely familiar to me from much earlier in the night. Numbly, I realised this was the owner of one of the jackets hanging on the pegs in the room next door. These were the remains of the first doorman who ran after us just as Keisha and Teagan ushered us down into the Club, except that now, most of his skin, muscle and flesh had been pulled, peeled and scraped from his bones. I recoiled from the table, only to see there was another stripped carcass stacked neatly on the steel shelf below.

There was a sudden ringing clatter as my heel glanced off the side of a metal bucket on the floor. As I stumbled back I felt the contents spill out, splashing my boots, soaking warmly through the material of my jeans. When I looked down, the gory sight and stench of spilt blood, folded innards and discarded eyeballs assaulted all of my senses in one full battery.

I felt my stomach begin to heave—but a further shock denied me the luxury of being sick. On hearing the metallic clatter, a familiar face suddenly shot up from the sliced mess of bone, flesh and gristle on the next trolley down. I had been so wrapped up in the revulsion and shock of the first trolley that despite its closeness, I had barely paid any attention to the second.

And in that moment, I realised the carcass on the second table was Gerry—his face still easily recognisable with most of the skin still in place, except for his lower lip and the exposed bone around his jawline. The head that suddenly appeared amidst his bones was that of Teagan. As she drew herself slowly upwards I saw she was naked, at least to her waist, and she was holding what looked like the missing piece of flesh from Gerry's face in her mouth, excess blood trickling gruesomely down her chest and belly. There were roughly smeared red stripes across her face around eye level—presumably blood—which gave her an aggressive, tribal appearance—the same markings I had seen on the mask on the wall outside the Club. It looked as if she had been lying or squatting low alongside Gerry's stripped body in amongst the gore and residue.

With her eyes now on me she spat out the flapping remains, pouted and smiled teasingly, arching her back slightly to accentuate the swell of her breasts—the trail of blood now looking perverse as it flowed down her front.

"Mmmm... It *is* an acquired taste, but so gorgeous raw," she said slowly. Steel glinted as she raised a small carving knife and nimbly sliced a thin strip of flesh from Gerry's frontage. She held my gaze as the meat snagged in coming away from his chest where the nipple held fast—then looking down with an air of indifference, she flashed the blade again and sliced through the offending piece of meat.

I was rooted to the spot in revulsion and fear.

"Oh, come on," she said enticingly, "don't look so shocked. You enjoyed your enemies earlier, wouldn't a friend taste even better?"

I began to feel the room move around me—my head spun with the horror of this and everything before. Despite everything I knew about self-preservation, I probably would have passed out on the spot had I not heard the movement of the door and the approaching shuffle of the Barman's feet behind me. Then I remembered the blood I had seen him dabbing away from around his mouth—and realised he was in on all this carnage with the rest of them.

With all the energy I could muster I forced everything from my head. To deal with it all I knew was that I had to be something I wasn't anymore. I took a sharp breath in and, lashing out with my clenched fist, I spun around and caught the Barman on his approach, the punch connecting fully in his face. I felt skin split under my knuckles as I connected somewhere around his nose, jolting his head suddenly backwards, sending his glasses flying into the air—a direct hit. I saw in an instant he was going down.

As he landed I took a wide step over him towards the door—only to see it pull away from me as I reached out for the handle. As the door opened I saw the hard features of Vincent beyond, the Medusa doorman, who was now standing immediately in front of me beyond the doorway in the anteroom.

In the instant it took Vincent to process what he was seeing, I launched myself directly at him, knowing I had to take him down quickly. But the sudden, instinctive push caused my balance to waver and I toppled forwards into him instead, my head connecting solidly with the area above his stomach.

Luckily, the unwieldly way I had fallen had shifted all my weight into the lunge. He reeled and fell backwards with the impact, buckling with the sudden winding. Lucky shot—but I was down too. For a brief moment we all lay dazed on the floor between the two rooms writhing in pains of one sort or another.

Then, probably because I was the most terrified, I regained myself, vaulted up and launched myself through the kitchen doorway, over Vincent's folding body and into the room beyond. I paused for a second to glance back to the kitchen only to see that Teagan was now completely gone with it all. She had returned to sprawling amongst Gerry's remains and had unashamedly taken to removing more of his flesh, working it with her knife and mouth. I couldn't watch any further.

I bolted across the room and out the second door back into the gloomy corridor where I had stood only minutes earlier, blissfully unaware of what lay ahead. The relief of bursting out of those rooms was overwhelming, like escaping from some vivid, vile nightmare, except I knew I hadn't actually escaped yet. And—Gerry was dead—murdered by these people for nothing more than...

I realised my clarity was going, images were beginning to seep through my thoughts, some of the other awful things I had locked away in my memory from a previous life that had nothing to do with this place. My own internal voice began to wonder if all the bad things I had managed to lock away, every horror I had managed to block to preserve my sanity over the years had now been released by those horrors in the kitchen.

I began to have intrusive flashes through my memory, tangles of massacred civilians in pits— butchered soldiers, most being no more than kids themselves—blood soaking into the sand in the ringing aftermath of exploded landmines... and then Gerry, lying dead in the next room—all the way back to that neither of us could shake, in the desert night when the girls began to scream, their final howls of anguish before everything stopped forever...

I had to survive this.

I inhaled deeply—seize it all—use the hurt—use the horror—harness the anger.

Focus you idiot, *focus*! I exhaled and forced everything out of my head—there was only one single objective now, and that was to escape, to live through this.

The darkness in the corridor was disorienting after the stark light of the kitchen, but I knew I wasn't far from the front doorway which, with Vincent gone, would presumably be unguarded. I decided it would be my best way out.

I bolted towards the ultraviolet glow which reached around the corner from the far end of the corridor. When I reached the reception area I saw there was no one there. My heart lifted as I saw the bar across the front door looked as if it had just been laid over the fixings with nothing to lock it in place.

But just as I was about to vault the final steps and haul the bar back, the double doors of the Club were thrown open by Pierre, who immediately stopped in his tracks to glare at me. The look on my face could only have told him that the secret was out. He snarled like an animal, baring his teeth and began stalking towards me, hands and fingers tensed and wavering like snakes, forming claws tipped by those sharpened fingernails I saw earlier—he was ready to slice.

I had to move fast but there were precious few options. Even though they looked flimsy, I grabbed hold of the closest wooden chairs at the desk and charged at him full on, its legs raised up and forwards.

As the wood connected, I felt his strength as he pushed back hard—but I managed to get enough momentum into it to slam him hard against the doors behind. It wasn't enough to put him down but he was off balance and stilled, if only for a few brief seconds.

I knew he would recover quickly, so there was no time to work on moving the bar—and it looked as if the only route out of the reception area was the direction from which I had come.

I spun around, vaulting off back into the corridor, hoping neither Vincent nor the Barman had recovered enough to get themselves back out of that room yet. With as much strength as I could find in me, I broke into a run.

Within a few seconds I was approaching the door to the kitchen anteroom. As I approached, I saw light began to spill out from it—it was slowly being drawn open. I dug in deeper; I knew if anyone came out of there ahead of me it would be another fight. I passed it whilst it was still opening, resisting all temptation to look inside, focusing instead on the darkness of the corridor ahead, praying it would offer me some other way out.

12. Flight

I hadn't covered as much ground as I wanted before I lost all semblance of light. For the first time, probably ever, I began to regret not having a mobile phone, even if only for the torch. My run had now slowed to more of a cautious walk and the only thing around me now was a sense of overwhelming blackness and the sounds of my own movements reflecting back at me.

I began to feel my way forward with my fingers along the walls, trying to avoid tripping by carefully pushing my toes out and forward with every step. I knew it was dangerous, moving deeper into a place I couldn't map or be sure of retracing my steps from—but at that moment there were no other options.

Before long the seconds turned to over a minute, and then I realised by the apparent openings that the open corridor appeared to diverge into a series of connected chambers. I realised I could only have seen a fraction of the floorspace of the building in the Club area. It was probably safe to assume this cellar level sprawled the entire footprint of the building which, from my memories of the outside, was substantial. But in the dead gloom my eyes seemed to adjust surprisingly quickly.

It was odd, I wasn't aware of any light source, but all the same I realised I was beginning to pick out vague shapes in the dark—openings in walls, rubble piles, ridges underfoot where the floor was uneven. Somehow it was becoming easier to judge distances and to see whether the archways which punctuated the walls were either cellar alcoves or openings to other open areas. I reasoned this could only have been the adrenaline boosting my senses in my heightened state.

Stilling myself, I listened for any sounds of pursuit. There were none—or at least none yet. I exhaled deeply—in the space of only a few moments it had become clear that now, everything was at stake. I had survived some sick situations over the years, but nothing like this. Even so, I knew only too well how these scenarios worked; what I had already seen would most likely mean the death of me should I allow myself to be captured. I was a loose end, a huge risk to everything they were doing, whatever insane thing that might be.

Pulling one of the candles out of my pocket, I struck a match on the bare stone wall and lit it up. Almost immediately, all the vague impressions sprang vividly to life, even in the poor light of the candle flame. There wasn't much in that particular vault to speak of—a few empty crates here, some discarded newspapers there and a clutch of empty, grimy beer bottles piled in one corner. I saw one single archway ahead of me in the far wall and briskly walked through it. I still had no clear plan, but at least if I was constantly moving forward then I should be putting more distance between myself and whoever might come after me.

I moved through the next empty chamber towards what appeared the next exit on the following wall. Walking slowly so as not to put the flame out, I was aware the smell of damp stone was growing stronger—but still there were no doors or windows anywhere, no hint of escape I could see. I had to think of something, I reminded myself again that my life depended solely on getting out of there.

Debris and dust crunched underfoot as I moved through the labyrinth as carefully as I could. The next chamber was much the same—and the next—and the one after that. Some had two exits, some only one.

I realised that in the haste of escape, those first moments where I blindly ran through the corridors and chambers beyond the kitchen had cost me my precious sense of direction. To make things worse, I could also tell from the constant muffled level of the thumping disco that I still seemed to be far too close to the main area of the Club no matter how many rooms I passed through. I began to suspect I had probably been walking around in wide circles in the dark.

Eventually I stopped in a room where there was a suggestion of light ahead. I stepped through the connecting archway and saw distinct shafts of coloured light, horizontally beaming across the room. Around the halfway point on the wall to my right I saw there was a large, bright rectangular grid of projected light. It took me a few seconds to work out what I was looking at. I blew out the candle.

Tracing the beams of light back to their source, I saw there was a metal grate set in the wall around eye level to my left. This seemed to be an air vent of sorts into one of the farthest walls in the Club, through which the streams of light and sound beyond were escaping. My breathing still laboured, I edged around the wall to the side of the grate and peered through.

The vent was big enough to see past what looked like two or three layers of brick and then into the main part of the Club beyond. From what I could see in the restricted view, it seemed this was one of the alcoved recesses beyond the dance floor. I flexed up on my toes and found that if I looked down I could see a partially obscured table littered with wine glasses and cigarette packets. There were shapes around the table of at least three diners, possibly more.

As I stood there the music lulled, allowing the sound of their chatting and conversation to became more audible. But then the music resumed, detail in the voices fell away as the trancelike intro began to an Underworld anthem, a track that meant so much to me back in the day. The memories it brought back were strangely exhilarating and out of context.

Looking through this window into the Club, it was as if I could feel the music even more intensely, as if my connection to everything in here—the people, the lights, the music—was hardwired somehow. There was little else I could do as I listened as the intro played out and the relentless tribal bass drum began. When it did, I felt as if every beat pulsed through me, as if each kick was some kind of short energy burst reaching out and into me from the next room—the sensation was overwhelming.

I turned around and flapped back to rest against the wall. Straight away I felt my body catch up—my head began to spin, my stomach spasmed. All at once the grim scene in the kitchen, the fight from earlier on, every horror from the past and the realisation that I had just lost a friend to these butchers all combined with the thought of what (or who) was now inside my stomach from the meal earlier. The message came through hard to my gag reflex—my guts convulsed and I finally threw up.

I buckled to my knees bending over close to the ground to try and stop the noise from carrying. The pain in my stomach racked my whole body and it felt as if every nerve was straining with the effort.

Then, after a few brief seconds, it was over. Thankfully, in the darkness at ground level I couldn't see the detail in whatever I had puked. I wiped the tears from my eyes and pulled myself up to the vent again, doing my best to avoid standing in my own sludge. I tried to get a better look at who was sitting beyond, but the grate didn't afford a clear view.

Through the metal grid I could make out impressions of the diners sitting around the table. I saw the top and side view of a middle-aged balding man's head; he was slim and intense looking. I had a side view of a smaller, younger man with thick dark hair dressed in casual clothes and caught the occasional glimpse of a pretty girl with shoulder length dark hair in a black polo neck smoking a cigarette.

The grate seemed to be positioned partly above their heads so their conversation could be separated—with some effort—from the throb of the music beyond. I strained to listen and found I could pick out bits and pieces of their chat. They seemed to be gossiping about the other people in the Club.

"Well, I think it's a pretty poor show, myself," said the balding man. "The word is there wasn't enough to go around until the girls made that catch earlier. I say he's just not up to it. It's ironic really, nothing ever changes—just another incompetent French Captain."

"Oh, come on, Pierre's done alright in the past, and you've got to admit it's turned out well enough," said the man in casuals.

"It has been functional, but if it hadn't been for the girls it all would have been an embarrassment. All that distance and risk for nothing," Balding complained. "I'm quite sure he's winging it, I always thought as much."

"Fuck's sake, there's just no pleasing some folk, is there?" said Casuals. "I'm sure he would have had something else up his sleeve—he's a resourceful old bastard, our Pierre."

"Maybe, but it's not *traditional*, is it? I mean, what if there was going to be an Initiation or Ascension tonight? We would at least need a..."

Suddenly there was a whoop and cheer from the main part of the Club way beyond my line of vision. All three guests turned to look, then all clapped simultaneously.

"Yesss!" cheered the man in casuals. I had no way of seeing what had attracted their attention. After a few seconds the conversation resumed. This time it was the girl who led in a husky voice, "Hey, what does it matter anyway? As long as they check out, one Longpig tastes pretty much the same as the next, doesn't it?"

Balding took umbrage at this, "No, no, no, no!" he whined. "That's just missing the whole point!" I saw the skin on top of his head shake slowly in despair, "You'll understand once you've been part of this as long as I have—it's not only about the tasting of the meat - it's what you can *know* through it, the assimilation. These tastings should be treated with reverence, we're dealing with the frontiers of human experience here—*absorption* of forbidden knowledge, the blending of minds as well as the greatest taboo."

The balding man sighed, he looked as if he knew he was wasting his breath. "You know yourself the difference it makes—the senses, all the more sharp? The instincts, all the more pronounced? That feeling

of being able to reach out, of *knowing* through another? I mean, what's the point of it all if not to advance ourselves?"

"Oh yeah..." Husky Girl smiled mischievously and nonchalantly blew cigarette fumes into the air. She looked as if she didn't give a shit about the semantics or the drama.

"Aye, right," said Casuals and looked away, his attention now appeared to be drawn elsewhere.

Then it hit me—a belated trail of association. Those words I had heard Teagan whisper to Vincent when we first stepped into the Club: '*Cochon longue*.' French for pig and French for long. Pigs long. Long pigs. Longpigs. And... jeez, I knew this. There was a 90's band called The Longpigs—and I knew where the name came from—it was a bizarre piece of trivia that stuck with me, as these things do if they're morbid enough. Longpigs was the slang term that cannibals used for their prospective human food.

Shit. We were the Longpigs, we had been all along. It was unreal. I wondered if things might have been different if I had made the connection earlier—but then I would probably never believe that such a thing was possible in this bar—in this city—on this night.

"Anyway," said Husky Girl, "If it wasn't for that incompetent French Captain back in the day, the Olds would never have been on the raft, never ran out of food and never been driven to taste the others. None of us would be here if it wasn't for him,"

Balding said nothing, he was having none of it. Husky Girl finally raised her hands in surrender and shook her head, having lost interest. There was a brief pause as they all took sips from their glasses. "So, I see they've wheeled in the display table—what do you think the final floorshow might be?" asked the girl.

Balding shook his head despondently. He appeared to have taken a huff.

"Honestly, I've no idea," said Casuals. "But hey, when they do fill that table it'll be great!"

Balding shook his head, "It'll probably be some pathetic last-minute drama, knowing Pierre. I'll tell you, the next time it comes around to meeting in *this* town, someone else better be doing the organis..."

A different set of sounds suddenly interrupted the conversation - but these were coming from behind me rather than through the vent. There were footsteps approaching on the stone floor beyond the doorway to the chamber I was standing in. I judged they were probably beyond the previous chamber too. I had a two-room head start.

I moved quietly away from the grate and through the archway opposite, even deeper into the dusty bowels of the building. It now made me nauseous that all my senses seemed so receptive. 'All the more sharp'—it really was just like the balding guy said.

I paused past the archway just to make sure. Yes, there was no mistaking—those were definitely approaching footsteps and there was more than just one set...

13. Barred

I moved off again, this time picking up the pace. I passed through at least five or six further chambers, but frustratingly I never seemed to travel much farther away from the pounding rhythm of the disco, which always seemed to be just through the walls to my left. I probably still hadn't put much distance between me and the central part of the Club.

Then suddenly, unexpectedly, I had a break. I came to a room which had a choice of three exits and took a right turn, away from the source of the music. That led me into a larger, colder chamber. There didn't seem to be any arched exits from this room but at the far side I could see a flight of steps with iron railings, maybe four or five feet high which led upwards to a black recess in the wall.

At that time the movement of feet was still behind me—whoever was coming this way didn't seem to be in a hurry but they were getting closer all the same. I decided to light up another candle.

I struck up a match, touched the flame to the wick and again the whole room seemed to illuminate so I could see the features in the room in detail. The railings were part of a small stairway that led up to a cross-barred, double fire door with a large retaining bar across it—which presumably led to the outside. Hadn't Gerry said something about this bar having a door farther down the main street? Jesus, this could be it!

I dropped the candle and saw the outlines fade slightly. Two or three bounds took me up the stone steps. There were two lever type handles on the doors. I lifted each one in turn but they were already hanging, both were loose and disengaged, obviously long since broken. I felt my way around the edges and reasoned that it could only have been held closed by that one metal bar which was slid through the mounted brackets on the doors and walls.

There were no padlocks or bolts holding it in place that I could see. It appeared that all I needed to do to open it was to somehow slide that heavy bar out of position. I placed my ear up against the door and found I could hear noises from outside—the swish of car tyres on wet road and voices of probably the last of the clubbers making their way home.

I heaved at the door to see how strong it was and winced as a metallic rattle filled the room and the corridors behind. I realised straight away I had given my pursuers a beacon to follow in the dark. Feeling the urgency rise even higher, I looked up and realised there were sliding bolts at the tops of the doors anchoring each into the frame. I pulled at both in turn, and to my relief they easily turned and fell down into their sheaths. Again, I hauled at the doors—this time they gave partially outwards having now been released from two of their fixings—but there was still no sign of any give from that metal bar which remained stubbornly rigid across the middle.

I grabbed onto the bar and pulled hard as the sound of gathered footsteps moved one room closer, now crunching in the stone dust just beyond the room I hoped to escape from.

The bar didn't move. I felt a sharp, ragged pain and the warm sensation of blood in my hands as my fingertips shredded against the rusting metal.

"Fucking *fuck*!" I heard myself hiss in the cold, spitting the words out through the pain. I pulled again long and hard, gritting my teeth and putting my whole body into the effort. But this time the bar moved—it slid along a matter of two or three inches.

In the next room the footsteps slowed. They were joined by further footsteps, more bodies congregating. I became aware of the excited murmur of voices in the gathering crowd.

I pulled again, this time my hands slipped along the bar as it gave a little more. I heard a metallic snap as it fell free of the first metal fixing in the wall.

The excited murmur grew to occasional discernible words:

"*...can hear him through here, just at the old entrance...*"

"*...seems a tough one—his taste suggests an interesting past...*"

"*...but must have known he would never escape...*"

"*...who the hell does he think he is anyway?*"

"*...bloody arse...*"

"*...good sport though...*"

By then the palms of my hands had begun to lacerate as I clawed and grappled at the corroded metal—but it was paying off; the bar moved another few inches, almost freeing up one complete half of the door. For some reason I found the smell and taste of my own blood overpowering...

"*Aha! There he is!*"

They were now beginning to enter the room behind me.

A final push—I threw everything I had into it, every last piece of drive and determination, using the fear, using the anger. The bar moved one last time and then stalled with a jerk—but one complete half of the door was now completely clear. Again, I pushed it hard—I needed to get this open, just wide enough to let me squeeze through it to the outside...

But my heart sank when the door held fast after the first couple of inches. The doors opened out just enough to let some streetlight shine in through the gap, making it easy to see there was still a solid hasp and padlock holding the doors fast together on the outside. In my own frustration, I screamed out of the narrow opening into the empty street for someone to come, someone to help, someone to get the police—but all I heard by way of reply was the echo of desperation as my voice reflected off the high stone walls opposite. The traffic I heard earlier must have passed, the homebound clubbers gone on their way.

A wash of despair consumed me and I felt everything drain, the anger, the fear, the fight, the will to survive. Everything I had known, everything that had kept me alive in the worst of times and places in the past had deserted me in that darkened cellar, in my own hometown, in the face of what I had seen these people do to others purely for their own self-indulgence.

I turned to face my pursuers and saw their shapes still gradually filling the room. I could see some of their faces, now amber lit by the streetlight from the gap in the doors behind me. It was as if they were all standing back in some sort of perverse anticipation, like voyeurs enjoying this final surge of despair as I finally realised they were right: there *was* no escaping this Club.

I heard the sound of a woman giggling lightly amongst the crowd. Turning around to the doors again, I threw my fingers between them in a final effort to prise them open while at the same time screaming as hard as I could—to apparently nothing and no one beyond.

I was still screaming when I felt the pressure of long, muscular arms from behind closing around my neck and torso. As I struggled best I could with the last of my energy, some sort of cloth was clamped over my mouth and I found myself overcome by the sickly-sweet tang of chemicals and antiseptic. Almost immediately, my head began to lighten and spin.

Resigned though I was, I still dug deep and struggled—I fought the best I could, even though I knew by then it was hopeless. After everything I had survived in the past there was no way I wanted to go out like this—but nothing seemed enough to shift those iron grips or lift the lightness in my head that was now draining my sight.

I felt my legs fail and my consciousness slip away to the sound of deep throated chuckling, and the scraping noise my boots made in the dust as I was dragged away backwards.

14. Floorshow

I seemed to come around in stages.

At first, I was comfortable and euphoric, I could easily have been in the comfort of my own bed at home realising this was all just some sick fever dream. But then my body began to wise up. My head hurt, my chest felt heavy and numb, my closed eyes were restless and painful, already hinting at the agony awaiting when I fully came to.

As the fog around my memory began to lift, I realised the source of pain in my head was a bright light shining directly above my face through closed eyelids. Piece by piece, my recollections returned and the vivid fear, horror and grief which had driven me just before passing out re-emerged, flooding through me as a sheer panic. I tried struggling dopily but felt little response from any part of my body. I became aware of voices chattering amongst themselves all around. Again, I found I could only make out snippets of what was being said...

"*...seems to be coming out of it...*" said the familiar voice of a girl I somehow knew.

"*...will be very interesting, what we'll learn from this one...*"

"*...not long now...*"

"*...and it's always much more fun when...*"

But again, everything began to fade. It seemed the more I faded away, the less pain and fear I felt—it was hard to resist, I didn't fight it. The voices around me began to dissolve as I drifted comfortably away to some distant, black place.

*

But it was a distant, black place from a previous life. I found myself again replaying the memory that seemed impossible for both Gerry or I to bury, no matter how hard we tried.

At first it was like a fleeting, sleepy memory that felt as if it might pass if I gave in to it—but something made me want to hold it there as I felt myself on the way towards losing all consciousness and presumably getting out of life for good.

In my anaesthetised, traumatised mind, I was back in that night on the Afghan plains yet again, in that rocky hollow, surrounded by the cold sand of the Dasht-e Margo desert, over three years later and three and a half thousand miles away.

The assignment had been unremarkable, but we knew there was a lot at stake. The local organised crime chief's wife wanted to defect. She was little more than a prisoner herself and probably saw the same for her girls, even if they lived long enough to grow up to be adults. Her proposition, which had been passed through a network of covert intelligence points, had been to tell us all she knew about her husband's operations, something which would be valuable in terms of saving lives—in exchange for extraction and guaranteed safety of her and her daughters.

At that point it had all gone to plan, even though she told us she was worried that her husband might be on to her. That night he was elsewhere, so security was lax and the few remaining guards were either sleeping or drunk.

Getting the team of four inside and then sneaking the family out of the compound had been relatively easy, there was no firefight, there were no casualties. Once we were far enough outside the walls, cursory searches were made and none of the family had any weapons. It was beginning to look as if the whole operation would be clean.

To get to the extraction site we needed to lead the wife and five youngsters up a steep, rocky trail outside their compound. This had mostly gone well, but it had distanced the party out due to some of them being unused to the climbing.

When we reached the top of the trail we stopped in a high rock enclosure, checked in, regrouped and did a headcount. That was the moment we realised that something wasn't right—we had one too many, we had more girls than we started with. We could only surmise this additional girl must have heard or seen us during the climb and decided to tag along.

It was entirely possible, even at night, there was always activity in the hills, they were rife with opportunists, spies and spotters for the Chief. His gang motivated entire families by keeping them in food, clothes, money, and promises that came 'straight from God'. They didn't care what generation did the work for them as long as it was done. So, young girl or not, everyone there knew how much risk this uninvited guest brought with her, especially if the Chief already suspected something.

Gerry caught on immediately and raised his weapon, but as we were all using night sights the dark clothing, the burqas and feint eyes all looked indistinguishable through the low light lenses—none of us could tell which girl was the imposter.

Straight away the mother realised the danger and began rallying the girls, shouting at them in Dari. Quickly the girls began to separate, as if they could sense one another other. Until, after a brief moment of panicked shouting and activity, one girl was left standing isolated and scared-looking apart from the group. We had options going forward—we could easily take her with us—but we needed to search her, assess and decide in quick time.

However, before a word could be said, the imposter girl slowly raised one hand high, clearly showing us that she was holding on to a hand grenade which was missing its pin. In a split second I recognised the shape, it was a British issue L109, small but utterly lethal at close range, potentially even through our layers of Kevlar. We had single figure seconds to act.

It was then the noise began all around. The girls began shouting in terror as they realised this infiltrator, who was no older than the rest of the kids there, was prepared to die in return for taking their lives—and ours—for whatever she may have been promised in the next world by the Chief or his cohorts.

There was no way to isolate her as we were in a natural surround, there was nowhere to run to, nowhere else to go. The shouting turned to screaming; they knew they were going to die. The surrounding rocks quickly magnified the cries to a deafening level.

Time slowed as I saw Gerry drop his gun, he bellowed at the family to get down as he dropped and tried to manoeuvre himself in an effort to shield them with whatever protection his body armour could offer—but the family seemed frozen, slow to react in the seconds they had left.

The two other young soldiers who had the rear of the party were still behind the girl. They looked around for cover in the limited space but only had the slender opening we had entered by. The seconds it took them to do this made them vulnerable targets. Standing on my own at what had been the head of the group, there was little I could do but throw myself down, feet pointed towards the grenade—as small a target as possible.

Then just before the sudden hot flash that ended the moment for us all one way or another, the time in my head seemed to stop—as if reminding me painfully of everything that was lost in the hollow that night.

Because of the high rock surround, everyone took the impact, either shrapnel or deflected rock debris. Gerry and I were a lacerated mess, shrapnelled and cut in every way possible. But we were lucky, we had dropped—the body armour took most of it at an angle and we lived through it—which was more than anyone else did.

Oddly, even as I felt the slow-motion light and pressure from the blast expand to take my consciousness away, it felt as if the screaming carried on into the darkness afterwards. The screaming was the first thing I remembered when I woke up, days afterwards in an allied medical unit, one of only two survivors.

*

Even at the time I knew all of it was a memory—but it still felt real. There was ringing in my ears, panic in my chest, and my body felt as if it were full of hot needles—all the grief, guilt and anger began to surge back. And just like that night in the desert, I could hear them all screaming again—there was no dulling through the medication I had been on since, no perspective of situation silencing them, and the passage of time seemed helpless in dulling the awful sound.

Right then they were all there with me, everyone was real again, standing right beside me, the terror in their screams still shrill enough to penetrate into my mind through the years and miles as I lay drifting around the edge of consciousness on that table in the Club.

I steeled myself and took a sharp, controlled inhale. I was still aware of where I was. I knew I had to fight back at the comfort of simply slipping away. The effort made me realise how much breathing hurt, it was like hammers pounding down hard about my chest.

Then, slowly, the bright light came back into focus above me. The gentle chatter in the room began to return to underpin the howling which filled my ears. I suddenly found I was able to move my own arms and legs in their bindings. I was returning, coming back into my body with the screams from the desert now at the front of my mind, dragging me back from that all too convenient, comfortable and pointless way out. My own terrifying ghosts had brought me back.

I knew it would hurt like hell, but I tried to make myself rigid. I breathed in deeply and exhaled, sending breath to every part of my body I needed to work with. Then, trawling up any reserve of energy, I fought the last of the blackness inside, gritting my teeth against the eager black cloud I had almost surrendered to. I heard myself moan with the pain as I flexed my arms and legs in an effort to restart my body.

"Ah, here he comes," I heard a male voice announce cheerfully.

"Oh, superb!" said a familiar girl's voice, Keisha.

Again, I moved, trying to struggle, but this time I felt firm resistance around my arms and legs.

I heard a gentle round of applause as I painfully opened my eyes and looked into the light above me—which was a square, overhanging box light—that looked as if it may have served over a snooker or pool table in a previous life. I lifted my head slightly and realised my predicament in an instant. I had been laid out on my back on some sort of freestanding table, tied tightly around my arms and legs in an arrangement that felt like binds connected beneath me. I was the floorshow.

As the polite applause continued, I realised my body felt cold, there was cool air drafting over my skin. At that point the light above my face was switched off and my surroundings fell better into focus. I lifted my head up as far as I could and as quickly as the glare from the light dissolved, I began to see shapes and colours fall into place around the room.

I saw I was undressed, the remains of my clothes lying in pieces on the table by my side, cut off with surgical care in situ, like some kind of casualty in a rushed emergency procedure. I moved my head from side to side and saw I was surrounded in this helpless state by almost everyone I had a memory of seeing in the Club since we first walked in. They were all smiling—as a group they seemed to be in some kind of happy state of anticipation.

Then the applause slowly petered out and stopped—but to my horror, the crowd stepped in closer towards me, eagerly watching, as if anticipating some other impending event. As the fear began to rise I tried to scream—but the sound I made never amounted to anything more than a choking gargle near the bottom of my throat.

I was aware of two forms approaching me from either side, familiar somehow, Gerry's anaesthetists, the men he had gone off to look for with Teagan just before they both disappeared. And then two unexpected sharp pains: one in my right arm, the other in the left side of my neck.

"Relax old boy, these will help you enjoy your part of the fun just that little bit more..." The voice was soothing, professional.

I felt the pressure increase beneath the pain and realised I was most likely being given some sort of surgical injections. I closed my eyes and tried to struggle in an effort to keep moving. Strangely, I felt a surge of adrenaline, as if my body were trying to fight the drugs being forced into me.

Then more fragments of detached discussions:

"...wonderfully clever you know, it isolates muscle movement but doesn't disrupt the sense of touch..."

"...dissolves in the stomach juices so it won't affect anyone's digestion—so there should be no nasty cases of heartburn afterwards..."

"...it's just so clever, what modern medicine can do..."

As my body became heavy everything around me became louder, brighter, more intense. It was as if I had lost all movement, but my other senses were heightening to compensate. Maybe even more so, if what the bald man said earlier was true.

Then, just as I reached a point where the colours and sounds were becoming overwhelming, there was a warm, fleshy sensation all over my body—a soft, perfumed smoothness that seemed to penetrate the pain, something warm brushed lightly over my face just before I heard Keisha's voice in my ear.

"*Don't worry, our two friends here know exactly just how much sedative you'll need, so you can still have fun too. We are going to enjoy you so much, my darling...*"

I shuddered as I felt the warm wet of her mouth trailing slowly from my ear down to my chest. Then a voice at the other side of my head, it was Teagan.

"*Relax, Lover—it's all becoming so much clearer—I'm beginning to see it all now—and it's all so sad. I can tell, you know—just like I could taste all the music in your past. It seems some things really do run in the blood..."*

I felt the warmth of her mouth on the other side of my head as it began to trace down to where Keisha was lingering around my stomach. I felt perverse—disgusted with myself for feeling the pleasure they were giving me—and for wanting it to go on forever.

I was stalled. In my mind it even felt as if the screams of the desert girls were now petering out, as if they had spent all their energy coming back from my past and having come all that way through time and space, I had only let them down by not being able to fight hard enough.

It was understandable, why would distant ghosts or anyone else bother themselves any further? What was the point? What did I really matter? It was all over, all I could do was wait for the darkness to fall that one last time.

Teagan must have anticipated my questions and slowly kissed her way back to around my right ear.

"But you know *how much you matter—and you know why—you've seen what ties us all together..."*

I tried to speak, to plead, but could only manage a frustrating gasp in my throat.

"Tasting is a secret only the few can know—a secret that has pleasures and sensations and benefits you would never believe..."

I felt her hand stroke down the length of my exposed torso and writhed as I felt another sharp pressure, Keisha biting into the area around my groin.

I wished I could ask her what she meant, but by then the drugs had such a hold of me that I now couldn't make any sound at all.

"Sshhh, don't worry my darling, you don't have to speak. Let me just tell you. It's the flesh and the blood that gives the knowledge—the mind, the memory, the spirit—the flesh is only the vessel they flow through. Most believe sex is the closest two people can be—but believe me, there's so much more. To truly taste someone, to have them dissolve inside you, for two to

literally become one, to feel the thoughts and sights, the sounds and desires of another life mingle with your own. Here, just look..."

Teagan gently slipped her hand behind my head and tilted it up so I could see down the length of my own body,

"How do you think I can hear what you're thinking? How do you think it is that my voice is inside you amongst all your other thoughts?"

I looked down and was met by the sight of Keisha, barely clothed and lying spread across the numbness of my legs, her face bloodied with the same tribal smear I had seen across Teagan's eyes earlier. Her head was level with my stomach, traces of thick, dark blood stained her mouth and upper body.

In her left hand she held a glinting surgical scalpel and, in her right, a long, bloody strip of my own freshly cut flesh. She looked ecstatic as she flipped her head back and devoured the flesh raw. As Teagan lifted my head higher I could see a large section of my chest and stomach had already been carefully carved away—a tangle of transparent tubes fed directly into the open wounds around my torso from a collection of drips and bags which hung suspended on metal stands by the table.

My stomach, almost comically, was lined at both sides with salad, sauces and garnishes from the table spread earlier in the night.

Teagan then cradled my head so I could face her again and in my sheer terror I saw her smile, genuinely—wide and loving. As she bared her teeth, I saw a small sliver of meat drop from the side of her mouth.

"Just think, Lover," she whispered. *"Soon I'll know all you've ever been or dreamed of..."*

I tried to snap my head back in the horror of it all but nothing was working, nothing inside my body was listening. I was aware of Teagan gently laying my head back down on the table, which now felt soft and insubstantial around my head.

It was then that my own mind began to scream, but my body couldn't follow. I felt the soft sensation of Teagan's skin retreat down the length of my body to continue the work she had already begun.

But as I lay dissolving into my last moments, I became aware of something else in the room. Suddenly there were different sounds, voices that seemed out of place. Then my mind snatched a final fragment of puzzled words from the air just before it shut down completely, "*How the hell did* they *get in here...?*"

15. Dead?

Those last few seconds were a confusing blur, it was difficult to separate the real sounds of the room from the separate streams of words now forming in my own mind. I felt crashing noises around me and the soft, warm pressures suddenly lift from my body. Then I sensed a sudden change, a rush of fear and panic connecting everyone in the room, jumping from mind to mind like static.

There was a sensation of urgency, a movement of air and then the draining of peripheral colour as my audience hastily departed.

Suddenly there were different sounds and thoughts in the room, which became stunted gasps and orders being given, the sound of feet moving quickly, heavily and efficiently. I was surrounded by new voices, a different audience and an overwhelming sensation of horror and disbelief all around.

I was aware of strangers shouting into my ear, asking me, somewhat stupidly, if I was okay and if I was in any pain. I tried to move some part of me, to give some sort of response—but there was nothing left, it was as if I were tightly locked inside myself. Then there was a sense of upwards motion, of all sensations around my body being released. I remember passing into an acidic tinged, dreamless void as the new voices in both the room and my head became all the more distant.

As the dark silence came, I honestly believed I had escaped the Club and everyone in it.

*

So how can I be here telling you this? Am I dead? Is this one of those stories where the narrator turns out to be an unreliable ghost? Or, did I finally wake up in bed to find it was all just some kind of night terror? I wish.

103

No to all the above. The truth is, I'm not exactly sure myself what happened next. After the Club, my next memory was of a bright room and hearing vaguely distorted voices of what I imagined were either doctors or police giving me snippets of unwelcome information, as if probing for some sort of response.

Again, all their conversations sounded patchy:

"...after we were told someone was trapped in the old nightclub..."

"...you sounded like the men we were looking for..."

"...we had never seen anything like that up close..."

"...they all vanished like rats down drains..."

"...it was almost as if they could see in the dark..."

"...they seemed to anticipate everything before we did it..."

"...you were lucky—just on the brink..."

"...we've never known anyone to survive after..."

"...seemingly..."

So, I guess that what I'm telling you is that right now—I'm not dead. I must have somehow mattered enough to someone to get me out of there before I bled out.

I'm guessing I'm in some sort of recovery—but I don't know where or how I got here, no one has explained that one yet. Maybe I was heard when I first screamed out of those fire doors? Maybe some of those drunken clubbers in the Cowgate heard the commotion and broke in? It could have been possible, especially with everyone inside distracted by the floorshow. I expect the authorities or whoever wouldn't have been too far behind—but those footsteps I had heard sounded purposeful, tactical—almost military—but I don't have the impression that I'm in any military place now—everyone here seems too measured, too presentable.

From what I think I've heard amongst the drifting snippets, it also sounds as if none of the diners were caught that night, although I suppose that isn't a huge surprise, considering the labyrinth I passed through trying to escape the Club. If even one of them knew the layout, they could have led the rest out elsewhere on the block before anyone realised what was happening—the same tactic Gerry and I used to escape the mob from Lady's.

Anyway, whoever found me would probably be too numb from the sights of the buffet to want to chase those particular culprits down into the darkness. Probably for the best, I don't want anyone else's blame for how that could have ended. It was bad enough that after everything Gerry and I had learned the hard way, we were still only too happy to fall into that expertly timed honey trap purely because it suited us. In a way I suppose it serves us right for believing any of their bullshit. What did we matter to anyone in that Club anyway? Who cared about us really? The truth is we were nothing to them other than fodder. If any of them did care, it was only as much as you might care yourself for the quality of your own next meal or evening's entertainment.

But that's all history now. To be honest I'm not much good at getting to grips with what's happening outside my head these days—and even then, I'm not sure I really want to anyway.

Even if they do save the parts of me I occasionally hear them talking about, even if they do get me back to 'mostly functioning' again, I doubt I would ever have a mind quiet enough to enjoy any sort of life again.

You see, since I've come in here I've had two regular visitors.

Not to my room—not visitors in that sense—visits to my mind. They still talk to me, they know what I'm thinking of. They seem to know all I've ever been or dreamed of.

"And soon Lover, we're going to do it all again. This time—Berlin!"

Oh God, they're here again.

"Pierre has found the most wonderful place this time around!"

"Keisha..? Teagan..? *Is that you..?*"

Club Medusa will re-open soon...

16. Based on True Stories:
A Brief History of Club Medusa

This story has been with me in one form or another for more years than I would like to admit. So, with the Club and me having such a long-term relationship, I thought it might be worth putting a few words down about the true (and maybe not so true) stories and inspiration that brought it all to life.

Club Medusa originally began life as part of a much bigger project I began in the late 90s. It was a standalone tale (originally called Club Batak) written alongside a number of others, all intended to be part of one big book with a connecting story arc through it. I wanted this big book to be like one of those old Amicus horror movies, preferably with Peter Cushing in charge, a group of seemingly random people telling their own stories in some way—then at the end, a punchline, usually something like, "What? We're all actually dead already? *Nooooo...!*"

Well, my punchline was weirder than that, but you get the idea. The whole 'big project' was good fun and a lot of work at the time—but to be honest, it all became a bit convoluted as I ended up having to alter and ditch ideas to make everything fall in line with the overall plan.

Long story short, I completed the manuscript—but it was rejected by every publisher who bothered to look at it. I did get some encouraging comments about my writing at the time from people in the business, but it wasn't long before I had a bad experience with an agent—and then it all stalled. This created a void which was quickly filled by the day job and then children. Next thing I knew, everything I had written was on a shelf gathering dust.

Fast forward to a serious return to writing last year which began with a review of everything I had written previously to see if anything might still fly. So, as I re-read that original huge manuscript, besides cringing in a lot of places, I did find that both Club Med and another story, Joey by David, still jumped out as being pieces I was pleased with. It didn't seem right just to forget about them and plough into something new.

And so, with a bit of editing, tightening up some vagueness and bringing everything up to date (for example, there were no mobile phones in the original—now the damn things rule our lives), the story developed into this version you have just read.

As to where the specific idea came from, that's all a bit trickier to explain. I seem to remember three different sources, all things that were in my head at that time. The first was a bizarre magazine article I'd read back then about 'Cannibal Rats.' This piece described some 'scientific' experiment where lab rats were taught how to navigate a maze, were then killed, and then had their brains fed to a bunch of new rats who, bizarrely, were able to navigate the same maze, seemingly without being shown the way. Oooh, ingested intelligence through eating educated brains? Yes, it sounds like total B-movie nonsense—and I can't find any source or trace of the article online despite the amount of tosh on Google—but the idea stuck with me due to the excessively grotesque weirdness.

My second source of wholesome inspiration was probably a number of escapades I had around that same certain time in my life when I still spent many a night partying in town with friends and colleagues. Although I'm no angel, I've never really been a competitive drinker, so I often found myself being the voice of comparative sanity at the end of the night trying to talk peers with alcohol induced high confidence issues out of blagging their way into Clubs and making arses out of themselves.

I didn't always succeed. In fact, I don't think I *ever* succeeded, but some of the hilarious and disastrous consequences did serve as part inspiration for this cautionary tale. Though I don't remember any of us being eaten back then. Well, not many of us.

The third thing was way duller and more conventional, almost the sort of thing a proper author would say, it was my lifelong interest in Edinburgh's history, especially the Old Town. When I was about eight or nine years old, my parents gave me a short book called The Ghosts, Witches and Worthies of the Royal Mile. I loved that book (I still have it) and all the great stories were there: Mary Kings Close, Deacon Brodie, Major Weir and his burning carriage, Half-hanged Maggie Dickson—all the scary greatest hits, and most of them happened in places I could go and visit—if I pestered my parents hard enough. Must admit, I've never really grown out of that—I still love strange local stories and visiting the places to soak up the vibes. Maybe that's a pastime that should have a proper name?

Anyway, that was one of the main reasons I wanted all the action to happen in and around the Cowgate. That part of town really is a hub for nightlife just like in the story, but at the same time, the nightclubs and neon bars are still surrounded by hundreds of years of history—and also not far from the scenes of many of my favourite grisly tales. I wanted the Old Town to play a part in shaping events and maybe also remind readers how much of a past there is down there when they're staggering back from the clubs after 3 a.m. And, if I could scare the crap out of some people along the way, that would be nice too.

It's maybe also worth mentioning, especially to readers unfamiliar with Edinburgh, that all the geography and place names mentioned are real. Most of the clubs were real too at some point—but most are just shoutouts to great places from times gone by. Shady Lady's, for example, the backstreet Club where Gerry and Paul end up brawling with the door staff, really was the name of the Club there in the late 80s. You would find Lady's (often with me and some of my chums in it) at the basement level of the nightclub complex in Victoria Street which over the years has been known as Nicky Tams, The Mission and

Espionage—and undoubtedly a few more before those. Shady's was at the very bottom part of the building and could be accessed directly off the Cowgate—almost a back door. It is also a fact that, although I have fond memories of the place, the clientele could be ropey at times.

Sadly, the whole complex seems to have closed down for good over the last year or so—the end of another era I suppose.

And then there's Club Medusa itself and all who sail in her. Okay, I made most of that up—but there are many bars and clubs in the Old Town you could easily walk into and believe you'd just stepped into the same venue as in this book. Many of the nightspots in that part of town really are old tenement cellar labyrinths with bare stone walls and bathrooms you may never find your way back from.

It's also true that there really is a large painting in the Louvre called Raft of the Medusa. Painted by Theodore Gericault in 1818-19—it's impressive, dark and terrifying, especially if you know the history. So, although they were being understandably vague, Teagan and Keisha were pretty much spot on. Also, back in the day, the story really was a big deal, and the French Captain really did get the blame along with the French King at the time for allowing the Captain's appointment.

I didn't want the characters to give a history lesson in the story, but to put the Medusa tragedy in perspective, over the 13 days drifting at sea, the 147 survivors on the raft from the shipwreck were reduced to only 15—and those who remained really did have nowhere else to turn but the only remaining food source. That's what I would call real horror.

My Medusans scattered at the end of the story, but if you ever feel the urge to visit the street where the Club was the night our heroes bagged an invite, the location is Merchant Street, west of Dyer's Close, just beyond the low archway supporting George IV Bridge.

Coincidentally, it's almost directly underneath The Elephant House Coffee Shop, where JK Rowling allegedly wrote some of the first Harry Potter book—which by my reckoning would have been written around the same time I was writing the very first sketchy draft of Club Med. How's that for a tale of contrasting successes?

Finally, back in the day when I originally wrote the first drafts of this tale, there was nothing beyond or below the iron railings where Teagan and Keisha are first seen other than steep, stone steps and a few dark and anonymous doorways. Believe it or not, there are now a couple of upmarket restaurants down there. I wonder what their specialty is. Do you think they do buffets?

In any case, I'll have a Chardonnay.

Martin White,
East Lothian (in Lockdown), April 2020

About the Author

Martin White has had an unusual career path - paper delivery boy, restaurant cleaner and coleslaw maker, print finisher, musician, police officer, photographer, author—some of those things were not like the others.

Originally from the Scottish fishing town of Musselburgh, he's spent most of his life living between there, Edinburgh and now a quaint village in East Lothian where there are more things lurking under its picture postcard surface than most people would like to believe. He's pretty sure there's a book in there somewhere.

With a lifelong interest in dark and macabre writing and anything else in life that's odd, surreal or just plain strange, he sets out to tell stories where unlikely and often terrifying things happen to normal people living their lives in ordinary places.

When he's not writing scary stories, he can usually be found reading or playing guitar somewhere.

Read more at www.martinwhiteauthor.com.